BYOMKESH BAKSHI

Saradindu Bandyopadhyay (1899–1970), the Bengali novelist, playwright and scriptwriter, is perhaps best-known for his immortal Byomkesh Bakshi stories, written in a span of four decades between 1932 and 1970. He was a master of several prose genres and wrote the award-winning historical novel *Tungabhadrar Tire* as well as screenplays for Bengali cinema and the Bombay Talkies. His major works include *Jhinder Bondi, Chiriyakhana, Jatismar* and *Bahu Juger Opar Hote*.

Monimala Dhar was born in Shillong and spent a major part of her school days there. Her late father A.M. Dam, an administrative officer of repute, encouraged and nurtured her love for Bengali literature. She has had a long academic career, serving as a teacher, a vice principal, a principal, and a chief administrative officer post retirement, at institutions of repute.

A 'compulsive' translator, she intends to make Bengali literature available to those who cannot access it in its original language. Her first volume of Byomkesh Bakshi stories came out in 2003. She has also translated Saradindu's reincarnation stories called *When the Earth was Young* and Abanindranath Tagore's *Rajkahini*. This is Monimala's fourth translated work.

BYOMKESH BAKSHI

Vol. II

Saradindu Bandyopadhyay

Translated by Monimala Dhar

Published by
Rupa Publications India Pvt. Ltd 2023
7/16, Ansari Road, Daryaganj
New Delhi 110002

Sales centres:
Bengaluru Chennai
Hyderabad Jaipur Kathmandu
Kolkata Mumbai Prayagraj

Copyright © Prabir Chakraborty
Translation copyright © Monimala Dhar

This is a work of fiction. Names, characters, places and incidents are either the product of the author's imagination or are used fictitiously and any resemblance to any actual person, living or dead, events or locales is entirely coincidental.

All rights reserved.

No part of this publication may be reproduced, transmitted, or stored in a retrieval system, in any form or by any means, electronic, mechanical, photocopying, recording or otherwise, without the prior permission of the publisher.

P-ISBN: 978-93-5702-222-4
E-ISBN: 978-93-5702-220-0

First impression 2023

10 9 8 7 6 5 4 3 2 1

Printed in India

This book is sold subject to the condition that it shall not, by way of trade or otherwise, be lent, resold, hired out, or otherwise circulated, without the publisher's prior consent, in any form of binding or cover other than that in which it is published.

This is our fiftieth anniversary. I want to dedicate this book to my husband, Pinaki (Prof. P.P. Dhar) for his tireless efforts in typing and editing the stories and of course, for bearing with me for half a century!

Contents

1. Money Matters — 1
   Arthamanartham

2. The Tantalizing Tarantula — 41
   Makorshar Rosh

3. A Thorn in the Flesh — 59
   Ponther Kanta

4. The Dart of Death — 100
   Agnibaan

5. The Vanishing Trick — 132
   Manimandan

6. The Bloodline — 156
   Rakter Daag

7. The One and Only — 200
   Adwitiya

Acknowledgements — 223

1

Money Matters
Arthamanartham

It was nearly lunchtime when the telephone rang in the next room. Byomkesh received the phone. I heard, 'Hello, Bidhu babu. What? A murder? You want me to come? We will reach within half an hour.'

Byomkesh slipped into his kurta, and while coming out of the room said, 'Let's go. There has been a murder. Bidhu babu has summoned us.'

I stood by, 'Which Bidhu babu? The Deputy Commissioner?'

Byomkesh smiled and said, 'Yes. I don't think he is calling me on his own—it must have been an order from the higher authorities.'

We had come to know Bidhu babu in the course of our work. A great know-it-all—he gave a lot of solemn advice to Byomkesh whenever we met, hinting that Byomkesh was much inferior to him in both efficiency and intelligence. Byomkesh listened to his lectures with great humility and laughed at him behind his back. The gentleman often divulged many police secrets while boasting. So whenever Byomkesh wanted some information from the police, he went to Bidhu babu and humbly listened to his lectures.

Anyway, after gulping down some food, we headed out. We reached our destination in twenty minutes by bus. The place was in the northern part of the city. It was a middle class, cultured Bengali area. While looking through the numbers of the houses, we noticed two policemen standing at a doorway looking this way, and that too in an alert manner while twirling their moustaches. We realized that this was the house. The constables let us in when they heard Byomkesh's name.

Although it looked like a small house from the outside, it seemed to be the house of a well-to-do person on the inside. As soon as we entered, we saw palm trees in pots lining the open space. On one side was a huge aquarium. Three sides of the building were occupied by rooms with verandahs. Just opposite the entrance, a staircase branched off leading to the first floor.

A room to the right was crowded with people. We saw that in the centre of the room, our plump, grizzly-moustached Bidhu babu was sitting at a table with a frown. The servant had already given his statement, and now it was the cook's turn. The man was standing with folded hands, tearfully answering Bidhu babu's harsh questions. He was shivering with fright as he was being scolded frequently. A few constables were standing around them.

Bidhu babu's face became more unpleasant when he saw us. He said, 'So you have come. Sit down. It is a very simple case. It is obvious who the culprit is. I have even issued a warrant in his name. But the boss asked me to call you...so I had to. You can also see what you can do, even though there is nothing to do.'

Byomkesh said, 'Since you have taken up this case, my presence is quite unnecessary. But as the Commissioner has asked me to investigate, I will work as your assistant. Could you tell me what happened? Who has been murdered?'

The power of flattery is unlimited. The god was pleased! He said, 'The master of this house, Karali babu, was murdered in his sleep. The modus operandi is a bit novel, and so my boss was quite nervous. But the crime is very simple. A nephew of Karali babu, Motilal, is the culprit. He is absconding.'

Byomkesh said with great humility, 'If you don't explain everything from the very beginning, it becomes difficult for a person like me to understand anything. Could you please tell me everything clearly?'

All his hesitation vanished and Bidhu babu said with a superior smile, 'Sit for some time while I take this man's statement, and then I will explain everything to you.'

The cook was still trembling. Bidhu babu screamed at him, 'Be careful. If you utter a single lie, you will be thrown in jail. When did you see Motilal babu leave the house last night?'

'Sir, I didn't check the clock. It must have been one or two o'clock.'

'One or two! Think and tell me the exact time!'

'Sir, twelve or one.'

Bidhu babu shouted, 'Why are you changing your statement? When—twelve or one or two?'

The poor cook swallowed hard and said, 'Sir, twelve.'

A constable wrote down everything.

'Did he go out quietly like a thief?'

'Yes Sir, he goes out every day like that and does not return home at night.'

'Don't talk unnecessarily. Respond only to what is being asked. Did you see Motilal babu coming down from the first floor?'

'No Sir, I only saw him going out of the main door.'

'You didn't see him coming down? Where were you then?'

'Sir, I... Sir, I...'

'Tell me the truth, where were you then?'

With a voice trembling with fear, the cook said, 'Sir, some

people from my hometown stay in a mess across the road. After I finish all my work at night, I go and chat with them.'

'So, you were there taking drugs with your friends, at that time?'

'Sir...'

'So the main door was open?'

The cook's voice seemed to dry up with fear, 'Yes, Sir!'

Bidhu babu looked at him with a frown and asked, 'Did you see anyone coming in or going out of the house?'

'Sir, no one went out of the house.'

'When did you return?'

'Sir, I came back within half an hour of Motilal babu's departure. I bolted the door; Sukumar babu had come in earlier.'

'What? Where did Sukumar babu come back from?'

'I don't know, Sir.'

'When did he return?'

'About twenty to twenty-five minutes after Motilal babu left.'

Bidhu babu's frown became deeper. He thought for some time and said to the cook, 'You may leave now. I will call you again, if needed.'

Bidhu babu looked at us, 'Did you see how all the facts came out in one interrogation? Anyway, you will only understand if I explain from the beginning.'

Bidhu babu told us that the murdered master of the house, Karali babu, was a wealthy, childless widower, with four or five houses in Calcutta and a few lakhs in the bank. He had many dependants living under him. His three nephews—Motilal, Makhanlal and Phanibhusan were the sons of his sisters, while Sukumar and Satyabati were the son and daughter of his deceased wife's sister. The over sixty-year-old Karali babu suffered from arthritis, was confined to his room and had a terrible temper—a fallout of which was the strange habit of changing his will at the drop of a hat. Three wills were recovered from his cupboard. In the first one, the beneficiary was Makhanlal, while in the second, it was Motilal. In the last will made the night before, Karali babu had given everything to Sukumar.

He would change his will whenever he was displeased with any of his dependants. The day before as well, precisely at noon, Motilal and the old man had a big fight about the will. Motilal was a man of many a faults, including a penchant for using abusive words. That he had left the house rather quietly at midnight was confirmed by both the cook and the servant, and Karali babu was found dead in the morning. There was something remarkable about the mode of the murder, and that it was discovered by the Deputy Commissioner himself: A needle had been pushed right into his neck, between the medulla and the first vertebra. The way he was murdered reminded Byomkesh of *The Bride of Lammermoor*, a story by Sir Walter Scott.

He thought for some time and asked, 'Have you issued a warrant against Motilal? Does he do anything? Could you get any news about him?'

Bidhu babu said, 'Nothing, he studied only till the primary classes. Totally spoilt, lived off his uncle and wasted his own time.'

Byomkesh followed up, 'And Makhanlal?'

'He is also like his elder brother, but not as spoilt. He takes cocaine and opium, but he is not as rotten as Motilal.'

'And what about Phanibhusan?'

'He is lame. He is not so bad; but that's because he is lame, and so, immobile. He cannot go out of the house. Of the three brothers, Phanibhusan is the best.'

'Sukumar?'

'Sukumar is a good boy. He is in the final year of medical college. His sister Satyabati studies in a college as well. Both of them used to look after the old man.'

'They are all unmarried, I suppose?'

'Yes, even the girl.'

Byomkesh stood up, 'Now let's see the house. Have you transferred the dead body?'

'No,' said Bidhu babu as he got up unwillingly. We followed him. Two flights of stairs led to the first floor. We saw a door just below the stairs. Byomkesh asked, 'Whose room is that?'

Bidhu babu said, 'That's Motilal's room. He preferred to sleep on the ground floor. The master was a very strict person who didn't allow anyone to go out after nine at night. He used to sleep directly over this room.'

Byomkesh pointed to another room in the corner, 'Whose room is that one?'

'That is Makhanlal's room.'

'Are they all in their own rooms, except for, of course, Motilal?'

'Of course! My strict orders are that no one is to leave one's room. There is a constable posted at the main door.'

Byomkesh praised Bidhu babu in an overwhelmed voice.

The room just in front of the stairs, on the first floor with a shut door, was Karali babu's room.

Byomkesh bent down in front of the room and said, 'What is this mark?'

Bidhu babu also bent down to take a look and straightened up to contemptuously say, 'It is only a tea stain. Satyabati used to bring tea for Karali babu every morning. Today, when she didn't get any response, she went in to find him dead. The tea must have spilled during that time.'

'Was she the first to discover the murder?'

'Yes.'

Karali babu's room was a mid-sized one. There were only a few pieces of furniture. But those few were neatly kept. On the left side of the room was the bed. It seemed that someone was sleeping sideways on it, with a cover on top. There was a table next to the bed on which bottles of medicines and a measuring glass were placed. A water jug with a glass cover was on the floor near the bed. It was obvious that the master of the house was a neat and tidy person. It was difficult to imagine that this man, who was sleeping sideways on the bed, was dead and had actually been murdered!

An untouched cup of tea was still there on the small table. Byomkesh examined the cup for a long while. Then he said in a low voice, 'Half the tea is on the saucer and the cup is half empty—why?'

Bidhu babu thought it unnecessary to respond to this silly comment and stood looking out the window.

Byomkesh picked up the cup carefully. There was a greyish layer on the surface of the tea. He stirred the tea and sipped it with a spoon. Then he placed the cup on the saucer, wiped his lips, and stood by the bed. He looked at the body for some time and asked, 'I hope no one has moved the body from its original position.'

'Yes,' Bidhu babu answered while still looking out the window. 'Only his head and face are covered with the sheet, and I have taken out the needle.'

Byomkesh removed the sheet slowly. The thin and wizened man seemed to be sleeping. There was no sign of pain or suffering on his face.

Byomkesh closely examined the dead body without moving it. He looked at the back of the neck. He bent down to look closely at the nose of the dead body; this he did for quite a long time. Then he told Bidhu babu, 'You must have already examined the body very thoroughly. Even then, I want to bring your attention to two things. The needle has been pricked three times into the neck.'

Bidhu babu had not seen it earlier. Now looking at it, he said, 'Oh, that's nothing. The murderer could not find the right place between the medulla and the cervical vertebra... That's why he had to prick the needle thrice. Now, what's the second thing?'

'Have you noticed the nose?'

'Nose!'

'Yes, the nose.'

Bidhu babu saw the nose, and as did I. We noticed that around the nostrils, there were some black spots, something like a dry skin condition that was common in the winters.

Bidhu babu said in a sharp and taunting voice, 'He probably had a cold. That happens when you rub your nose frequently. What do you assume from this?'

'Nothing, nothing...now let us see the next room. That was probably his sitting room.'

In the next room, there is a table, alongside a chair, a typewriter and a cupboard full of books. Karali babu used to spend most of his time here. Bidhu babu pointed to the drawer in the table and said, 'The wills were found here.'

Byomkesh went through everything carefully and said, 'There's nothing to see here. Let's go to Sukumar babu's room. He is the heir to the dead man's property. Let me see the needle please.'

Bidhu babu took out an envelope from his pocket. Byomkesh took out the needle from it with his two fingers. It was longer and thicker than ordinary needles and looked quite a bit like a carpet needle. A piece of thread was hanging from it. Byomkesh looked at it wide-eyed and said, 'Strange! Very strange!'

'What?'

'The thread—can't you see the thread hanging from the needle? It is black silk thread.'

'I can see that. But what is so strange about thread hanging from a needle?'

Byomkesh looked at Bidhu babu, and then, as if ashamed, said, 'That's true, there is nothing to be surprised about. What are needles for but for threads to go in through the eyes! How stupid of me!' He returned the needle to Bidhu babu and said, 'Let us meet Sukumar babu.'

Sukumar's room was on the left side of the verandah. The door was ajar and Bidhu babu pushed it open. Sukumar was sitting at the table with his hands covering his face. He stood up quickly as we entered.

The bed was on one side of the room, and on the other side was a table with a chair. Nearby was a cupboard for books. Sukumar was about twenty-four or twenty-five years of age. He was good-looking and it seemed as if he exercised regularly. But because of the terrible incident in the house, he looked pale and unhappy. He looked nervous when he saw us entering the room together.

Bidhu babu said, 'Sukumar babu, this is Byomkesh Bakshi. He wishes to speak to you.'

Sukumar cleared his throat and said, 'Please sit.'

Byomkesh sat in front of the table. He picked up a book, *Gray's Anatomy*, and leafing through it, he asked, 'Where did you return from at midnight, Sukumar babu?'

Startled, Sukumar replied in an inarticulate voice, 'I went to see a film.'

Without lifting his eyes from the book, Byomkesh asked, 'Which theatre?'

'Chitra.'

Bidhu babu said in a stern voice, 'You should have told me this, why didn't you?'

Hesitantly, Sukumar answered, 'I didn't think it was important.'

Bidhu babu said grimly, 'We will decide what is important and what is not. Is there any proof that you had gone to Chitra Cinema Hall?'

Sukumar thought for some time and then pulled out a coloured paper from the pocket of his kurta, which was hanging on the clothes rack. It was the torn half of a cinema ticket. Bidhu babu kept it in his notebook after looking at it carefully.

While flipping through the pages of the book, Byomkesh asked, 'Was there any specific reason why you went to the night show instead of the evening show?'

Sukumar's face became pale, he said in a low voice, 'No, not really...'

Byomkesh said, 'Karali babu did not like any member of the house to stay out late; you must have known that.'

Sukumar had no answer. He stood with a guilty expression.

Suddenly, Byomkesh looked up at him and asked, 'When did you last meet Karali babu?'

Sukumar swallowed hard and said, 'At five in the evening.'

'Did you go to his room?'

'Yes.'

'Why?'

Sukumar said slowly in a controlled voice, 'I went to tell him something about the will. He deprived Moti dada and willed all his property to me. He had an argument with Moti dada at noon. I went to tell my uncle that I did not want his property and that he should divide it equally among all of us.'

'Then?'

'He threw me out of his room when he heard what I had to say.'

'You went out after that?'

'Yes, I went from there to Phani's room. It was late when I finished talking to him. I was upset, so I thought I would go and see a film. Phani also advised me to go. So I quietly went out, hoping that Uncle would not find out.'

Bidhu babu's expression said that he was totally satisfied with Sukumar's explanation. He said sternly to Byomkesh, 'Tell me what you are thinking, Byomkesh babu. Do you think that Sukumar is the murderer?'

Byomkesh stood up, 'No, not at all! Let's go to his sister's room.'

Bidhu babu said rudely, 'Let's go, but I think it is totally unnecessary to irritate a lady. She knows nothing; I have already asked her whatever needs to be asked.'

Byomkesh said with great humility, 'Of course, of course. But even then, if I could once...'

Just at the turn of the verandah was the girl's room. Bidhu babu knocked at the door. After half a minute, a young girl of eighteen or so opened the door. We entered the room hesitantly. Sukumar had followed us; he went in and sat on the bed, tired.

We looked at the girl before entering the room. She was tall, dark and slim. Her eyes were swollen from constant weeping, and her face was slightly swollen as well. So it was not possible to make out whether she was good-looking or not. Her hair was uncombed; she looked a picture of misery. I was annoyed with Byomkesh for disturbing this young girl. But Byomkesh seemed determined.

He greeted the girl and said, 'I will trouble you a bit, please don't mind. When such a terrible incident occurs in a house, one has to bear the grief and also the harassment of the police.'

Bidhu babu retorted angrily, 'Do not blame the police, you are not a policeman.'

Byomkesh ignored him and said, 'I will just ask a few questions. Please sit down.' He pointed to the only chair in the room.

The girl looked at Byomkesh with intense dislike, then said in a low voice, 'What do you want to know? I won't sit.'

'You won't sit! All right then, I will.' Byomkesh sat on the chair and looked around. This room was simple like Sukumar's. There were very few pieces of furniture—a bed, a table and a chair, a bookcase; and a dressing table with drawers was the extra bit of furniture in the room.

Looking up at the ceiling, Byomkesh asked casually, 'Were you the one who took a cup of tea to Karali babu?'

The girl nodded.

Byomkesh asked, 'Today, when you took the tea, you saw that he was dead, didn't you?'

She nodded her head again.

'You didn't know anything before that?'

Bidhu babu said angrily, 'Stupid and unnecessary question—quite foolish.'

Byomkesh ignored him and asked, 'Was Karali babu's door kept open at night?'

'Yes, no one in this house was allowed to shut their door at night. Uncle, too, followed this rule.'

'Really? Then...'

Bidhu babu lost his patience, 'Enough is enough. Please get up now. Don't harass the girl with foolish questions. You have no idea how to cross-examine a person.'

This time, Byomkesh's mask of humility dropped. He glared at Bidhu babu like a wounded tiger and said in a low and intense voice, 'If you keep on disturbing me like this, I will be forced to let the Commissioner know that you are trying to disrupt my investigations.'

Bidhu babu would not have been more astounded if he was physically slapped. He glared at Byomkesh for some time and making an incomprehensible sound, walked out of the room.

Byomkesh then turned to the girl and said, 'You didn't already know about Karali babu's death? Think before answering.'

In a stubborn voice, the girl replied, 'I have thought...no, I didn't know about his death.'

Byomkesh remained silent for a few minutes with a frown on his face and then asked, 'How many spoons of sugar did he take in his tea?'

The girl looked at him surprised and then said, 'Sugar? He liked more sugar in his tea, about three or four teaspoons.'

Like a gunshot came Byomkesh's next question, 'Then why didn't you put any sugar in his tea today?'

The girl looked pale and terrified as she looked around the room helplessly. She then took control of herself with great effort and biting her lower lip, answered, 'I must have forgotten... I wasn't too well from yesterday.'

'Did you go to college yesterday?'

She answered rebelliously, 'Yes!'

Byomkesh got up from the chair lazily and said, 'If you told us everything, it would have helped us, and maybe it would have helped you too. Will you tell me everything?'

The girl said quietly and firmly, 'I don't know anything else.'

Byomkesh let out a sigh. Till now, he was looking at a sewing box on the table while talking. He walked up to the table, pointed to the box and said, 'This must be yours.'

'Yes.'

Byomkesh opened the box. There was a half-finished embroidered tablecloth and a bundle of silk threads. He picked up the bundle and mumbled to himself, 'Red, purple, blue, black...yes, black...' He put back the bundle in the box and started looking for something. He opened the folds of the tablecloth and asked the girl, 'Where is the needle?'

The girl had stiffened with fear. She repeated, 'Needle?'

Byomkesh said, 'Yes, needle. You must be stitching with a needle, where is it?'

The girl opened her mouth to say something but couldn't. She ran to her brother, placed her head on his lap and began crying bitterly. Sukumar tried to lift her face up and said in a bewildered voice, 'Satya… Satya?'

Satyabati did not lift her face and continued weeping. Byomkesh came up close to them and said softly, 'You should have told me everything. It would have been better for both of you. I am not a policeman. Ajit, let's go.'

After coming out of the room, Byomkesh closed the door carefully and said, 'Now, Phani babu. That corner room must be his.' Byomkesh knocked softly. A young man of twenty-one or twenty-two opened the door. Byomkesh asked, 'Are you Phani babu?' He nodded, 'Yes, come in.'

As soon as one looked at Phanibhusan, it became obvious that he had some physical defect, but it was not easily discernible. He was well-built, but his face was thin and bony. Sorrows of past years seemed to have etched their lines on his face. As soon as we entered, he walked in front of us and pointed to a chair and said, 'Please.' It was then that we realized what ailed him. His left leg was abnormally thin, so he limped badly while walking.

I sat on the bed and Phani sat next to me. When Byomkesh told Phani that the police had Motilal as the prime suspect, Phani said with conviction that despite all his faults, his elder brother couldn't have committed a crime like murder. When Byomkesh pointed out that being dropped from his uncle's will could be his motive, Phani retorted that the same held true for any of them, as the whimsical Karali babu kept on changing the beneficiary in his will on the basis of his relationship with the person concerned at that moment.

When asked whom the old man might have liked or disliked among his dependants, Phani said that for him, Karali babu felt nothing more than pity laced with contempt. His handicap had shrunk Phani's world only to his books in a small room. But although Karali babu lacked human emotions in his heart, he still liked Satyabati the best.

Byomkesh said, 'I am sure you know that Karali babu has given all his property to Sukumar.' Phani smiled, 'Yes, I have heard that. Sukumar da is the most eligible person. But one cannot gauge my uncle's attitude from this. He was extremely whimsical and changed his mind fast.'

Byomkesh said, 'Since the last will is in Sukumar's name, he will get the property.'

Phani said, 'Does the law say that? I don't know. '

'Yes, the law does say that.' Then Byomkesh asked hesitantly, 'What will you do under such circumstances?'

Phani ran his fingers through his hair and looked out the window, 'I don't know what I'll do or where I'll go. I am not educated, so I cannot look for any job. If Sukumar da allows me to stay in the house, I will stay; otherwise, I'll have no roof over my head.' Seeing that he was near to tears, I looked away.

Byomkesh said casually, 'Sukumar babu returned home at midnight.'

Phani looked startled, 'At midnight? Yes, he went to see a film.'

Byomkesh asked, 'At what time was Karali babu murdered, can you make a guess? Did you hear any sound?'

'No, maybe late in the night.'

'No, he was murdered at midnight.'

Saying this, Byomkesh got up. He looked at his watch and said, 'Oh! It's 2.30 p.m. Let's go home, Ajit.'

A commotion was heard downstairs at that time. The next

minute, someone pushed open the door and said, 'Phani! Dada has been arrested!' He stopped abruptly after seeing us.

Byomkesh said, 'You are Makhan babu, aren't you?'

Makhanlal was terrified. 'I don't know anything,' he said, and rushed out of the room.

We went down to find that there was a lot of noise and confusion in the sitting room. Bidhu babu was not there; a police inspector had taken his place. The police had brought a crazy-looking hand-cuffed person who was yelling, 'Uncle has been murdered? I promise I know nothing. I am a drunkard and I spent my night in Dalim's house. Dalim will be witness to that.'

The Inspector was efficient. He was sitting lazily all this while. When he saw us, he said, 'This one is Bidhu babu's culprit. You can interrogate him if you wish.'

Byomkesh asked, 'Where did you arrest him?'

The sub-inspector who had arrested him said, 'From the house of a woman in the red-light district.'

Motilal began shouting again, 'I was sleeping in Dalim's house. Which bast...who is saying that I am lying?'

Byomkesh stopped him and said, 'You return early in the morning every day, what happened today?'

He gazed around like a madman and said, 'What happened? What happened? I drank two bottles of whiskey and went off to sleep—that's what happened.'

Byomkesh nodded his head and made a sign to the inspector who said, 'Take him away and put him in custody.'

Motilal, who was shouting at the top of his voice, was taken away from the room.

When Byomkesh asked the Inspector about Bidhu babu, he was told that the latter had gone home and would come back in the afternoon. Byomkesh decided that we should also leave and return only the next morning. In answer to his query, the Inspector told Byomkesh that only the rooms of Karali babu and Motilal had been searched, as Bidhu babu did not think it necessary to search the other rooms. There was nothing incriminating in Motilal's room. Byomkesh said that since Bidhu babu was not there, he would have to wait till the next morning to satisfy his curiosity about the wills of Karali babu.

We returned home. In the evening, Byomkesh drew a plan of Karali babu's house and told me, 'The room below Karali babu's is Motilal's. Makhan's room is next to his. Below Phani's room is the sitting room. That is where the policemen are stationed. The room below Satyabati's is the kitchen and below Sukumar babu's room is where the cook and the servant sleep.'

I asked, 'What will you do with this plan?'

'Nothing,' said Byomkesh, and started studying it with great concentration.

I asked, 'What do you think? Motilal is not the murderer, is he?'

'No. Rest assured he isn't.'

'Then who is the murderer?'

'That is difficult to say. If we leave Motilal out, then there are four of them left—Phani, Makhan, Sukumar and Satyabati. Any of them could have committed the crime. All of them have the same kind of motive.'

That took me by surprise, 'Even Satyabati?'

'Why not?'

'She is a woman...'

'If a woman loves someone dearly, she can do anything for that person.'

'But what is her motive? Karali babu's last will bequeathed everything to her brother.'

'You didn't realize something. A person, who changes his

mind so frequently about his will, could be finished off so that he would not be able to change his mind anymore.'

I was astounded. I did not think of the case from this angle. I said, 'So you think it is Satyabati?'

'I did not say that. It could be Sukumar. It could even be someone from the outside; but Satyabati is no ordinary girl.'

The whole affair was so complicated that the more I thought about it, the more difficult it seemed. At last, I asked, 'What conclusion did you come to after examining the dead body?'

'I realized that Karali babu was chloroformed before he was killed.'

'How did you reach to that?'

'He was pricked three times in the neck with the needle. If he was not chloroformed, he would have woken up. Do you remember seeing tiny marks outside his nostrils? Those marks were made by the chloroform.'

'Why was he pricked thrice?'

'The murderer could not find the exact spot in the first two attempts. But that is not the most important thing. What's strange is why the needle was still stuck to the neck. The murderer could have easily removed the needle and thereby removed all proofs.'

'Maybe the murderer was in a hurry and forgot to remove it. But how did you understand that the murder was committed at midnight?'

'That is my assumption. But if Satyabati ever tells the truth, you will realize that my assumption was correct.'

Byomkesh sat for some time staring at the ceiling.

'There was a book on Sukumar's table, *Gray's Anatomy*. Only a few lines were underlined in red pencil in one page of the book.'

'What was the meaning of those few lines?'

'That if the spot between the medulla and the first vertebra was pierced with a needle, it would mean sure death!'

I jumped up with excitement, 'What are you saying?'

'But quite strangely, I didn't find the red pencil on Sukumar's table.'

He suddenly got up and began pacing the room with a worried expression on his face. I was bursting with unanswered questions but did not dare to disturb his chain of thoughts. I knew how irritable he became when he was interrupted.

Before going to bed, he asked me a question, 'You are a writer, what's the Bengali version of a thimble?'

I was surprised, 'Thimble? The thing that tailors wear on their fingers while stitching?'

'Yes.'

I tried to give a few Bengali words for a thimble but failed to satisfy Byomkesh with those makeshift expressions.

☙

When I woke up the next morning, I found that Byomkesh had gone out. I was a bit annoyed, but I understood that there must be some reason behind his going out alone without me.

It was about eleven when he returned. He sat under the fan and lighted a cigarette. I asked, 'What happened?'

Exhaling the smoke slowly, he said, 'I went through the wills. The cook and the servant were the witnesses. Their thumb impressions were there in each will.'

'What else did you do?'

'I asked the police to search all the rooms of the house. But Bidhu babu is stubbornly refusing to do whatever I was asking for. So, I had to threaten him that if he didn't agree to search the rooms, I would complain to his boss—the Commissioner.'

'Then?'

'Then what? He is still hellbent on Motilal being the culprit.'

Byomkesh was quiet for some time and then said, 'The girl is very stubborn. She refused to speak. But all the clues of this mystery are with her. Let's see if Bidhu babu agrees to search the rooms; something may come to light.'

'What are you expecting?'

'Let's see. Maybe a cash memo from a medical store or a pencil, or... But it is no use speculating. Let's go and have our lunch.'

Byomkesh spent the entire afternoon relaxing in a chair, with closed eyes. It felt like he was waiting for something.

At four-thirty in the afternoon, the telephone rang in the next room. Byomkesh went quickly to receive the call.

'Oh, Inspector, what's the news? Have you searched Sukumar's room? So Bidhu babu agreed at last! What did you find in his room? A bottle of chloroform behind the books in his shelf? And a will? Another typed will? What is the date on the will? The day Karali babu was murdered? Where was it…under the trunks? Who is the beneficiary of this will… Phanibhusan? Right, it was his turn this time. Have you arrested Sukumar babu's sister? No? What else did you get from the room— nothing? Any red pencil? No? Strange! Found any stuff used for sewing—not even that? Is Bidhu babu there? Has he gone to release Motilal? That's good, he has come to his senses. Have you not searched any room other than Sukumar's? Oh, Bidhu babu did not think it necessary, did he? It seems that Bidhu babu does not think that anything is necessary! Do I need to go there today? I want to see the new will… Oh, Bidhu babu has taken it? Okay, I will go tomorrow morning. Till the time that red pencil and those sewing equipments are found, we can't say anything. What are you saying? Overwhelming evidence has been found against Sukumar? Did you get the medical report? What was the time of the murder? Three hours after dinner…

That is about midnight. Alright, I'll go there tomorrow.'

Byomkesh came back after the conversation. Looking at the frown on his face, I knew that he was not very satisfied. I asked, 'So it is Sukumar, after all. You suspected him right from the beginning…'

Byomkesh remained quiet for some time and then said, 'All the evidence points to Sukumar. The very way in which Karali babu was murdered seems to prove unmistakably that it is the handiwork of a doctor. Those who know nothing of medical science could not possibly kill in that manner. The needle with which the crime was committed was also stolen from his sister's sewing box; even the thread hanging from the needle was the same as that in the box. Sukumar came back home at midnight, and Karali babu died at that same time. After searching Sukumar's room, two things were found: a bottle of chloroform and a typed will—Karali babu's last will in which he gave everything to Phani. Sukumar himself admitted that he had fought with his uncle that very evening. So he knew very well that his uncle would change his will. Even the motive of the murder is clear.'

'So Sukumar is the murderer. Is there no doubt about that?'

'Do you think there is any doubt?' Byomkesh was quiet for some time, then he said, 'What do you think of Sukumar? Does he seem like a fool to you?'

I said, 'Not at all. In fact, he seems like a very intelligent fellow.'

Byomkesh said thoughtfully, 'That's why I am puzzled. Why did an intelligent person behave like a fool?'

Suddenly, Byomkesh became very alert. There were sounds of footsteps outside our door. Byomkesh called out, 'Please come in.' For some time, there was no response, then the door opened slowly. To my utter surprise, I saw Satyabati standing at our doorway.

She entered and shut the door behind her. She stood stiffly for some time and then suddenly burst into tears. In a choked voice, she said, 'Byomkesh babu, please save my brother.' She seemed under great stress and was nearly blacking out. She blindly stretched out her hand for help. Byomkesh jumped up quickly and led her to a chair. I increased the speed of the fan.

For a minute or two, Satyabati wept uncontrollably. Embarrassed, we looked the other way.

I had met Satyabati only once earlier and I didn't think that she was in any way different from other ordinary Bengali girls. I realized that she had abandoned all her fear and hesitation now, in the face of grave danger to her brother. I was under the impression that most Bengali girls froze when faced with danger. So I was impressed with this young girl for showing courage and coming to a detective on her own. I viewed her in a new light.

Satyabati wiped her eyes, lifted her face and said again, 'Byomkesh babu, please save my brother.' I noticed that she was trying her utmost to control her emotions, although her voice was still trembling.

Byomkesh said slowly, 'Your brother has been arrested. I heard about it, but…'

Satyabati said anxiously, 'Dada is innocent. He knows nothing, and he has been arrested without any reason.' She began crying again.

I understood that Byomkesh was moved at the sight of this weeping girl, but he said coolly, 'The evidence is against him…'

Satyabati interrupted vehemently, 'Those are all false. Dada can never murder anyone for wealth and property. You don't know him. Byomkesh babu, we don't want any property. Please help in getting my brother released; we will always be grateful to you if you do that for us.' Tears poured down her cheeks without her realizing it.

When Byomkesh spoke again, I noticed that his voice was filled with deep emotion. He said, 'If your brother really is innocent, I will put in every effort to try and save him, but…'

'Don't you believe that my brother is innocent? I will touch your feet and take a vow that he cannot do a thing like this. He cannot even harm a fly…' While saying this, she bent down to touch Byomkesh's feet.

'What are you doing? Please get up,' Byomkesh put his feet away.

'But you must promise that you will release my brother!'

Byomkesh pulled her up and made her sit on the chair again. Then he sat in front of her and said in a firm voice, 'You are making a mistake. I cannot release Sukumar babu; only the police can do that. I can only try. But to do that, I must know everything. Can't you understand that if you conceal anything from me, I will not be able to help you?'

Lowering her eyes, Satyabati said, 'I have not concealed anything from you.'

'You did. You knew about Karali babu's murder that very night, but you didn't tell me that.' Wide-eyed with fear, Satyabati looked at Byomkesh, then lowered her head in silence.

Byomkesh said, 'Will you tell me everything now?'

Satyabati looked at Byomkesh with pitiful eyes, 'If I tell you everything about that incident, the blame will come on my brother; so how can I tell you about it?'

Byomkesh said in a pleading voice, 'If your brother is innocent, then revealing the truth will not harm him in any way. Tell me everything and conceal nothing.'

Satyabati sat thinking silently for a long time. Then she said in a broken voice, 'Alright, I will tell you everything; there is no other way out for me.' She wiped her tears and spoke in a soft and controlled voice, 'That evening, my brother had an argument with our uncle. Uncle had given all his property to my brother in his last will. Motilal da had a big quarrel with Uncle about this at noon. When my brother heard about this after returning from college, he went to ask Uncle to divide the property among all of us. Our uncle could not tolerate any opposition to his decision. So he got very angry with my brother and said, "How dare you question my decision! Get out! I will not give you a penny." My brother had not realized that Uncle would be so angry with him. He came out of the room and went to Phani da's room. Phani da is lame and is unable to step out of doors, so my brother spends some time with him every evening. You must have seen Phani da. He has not studied in school or college, but he is very knowledgeable. If you have noticed the books in his cupboard, you will realize how many subjects he knows about. I go to him for explanations if I am stuck with something in my subject.

'My brother was unhappy after the argument with Uncle. He told me at about eight in the evening that he would be going out to see the night show of a film. He said, "I'll come back at half past eleven, please keep the main door open." Saying this, he went out quietly after dinner. Our cook stays up till late at night to chat with the people from his village, and so I didn't stay awake to open the door for my brother. At about ten, I went off to sleep.

'I had fallen off to sleep when I suddenly woke up. I thought I had heard a noise in my brother's room—something like a box or a table being pulled. I assumed that he had returned after the show.

'I tried to sleep, but for some reason I couldn't; so I stayed awake for some time. I heard no sound from my brother's room, and so I thought he had gone off to sleep.

'About fifteen minutes later, I heard the sound of footsteps tiptoeing across the verandah. I found it surprising; my brother had come home some time ago, then who is walking along the verandah? I got up from bed quietly, opened the door slightly and found my brother walking very quietly to his room. Moonlight was streaming into the verandah—I saw him clearly.'

Byomkesh said, 'Was your brother wearing shoes?'

'Yes.'

'Did he have anything in his hands?'

'No.'

'Nothing? A piece of paper or a small bottle?'

'No, nothing.'

'Did you notice what time it was then?'

Satyabati said, 'There was no need to notice, all the clocks of the city were striking midnight.'

Byomkesh's eyes became sharp with excitement, he said, 'Please continue.'

Satyabati continued, 'At first, I could not understand anything. Dada had come fifteen minutes back; I had heard come noise in his room. Then where had he gone now? I thought that since our uncle could not sleep sometimes from rheumatic pain, my brother must have gone to him to give him medicine. I, too, went out quietly to see how Uncle was.

'The door always remained open; I entered the room. The room was dark but I could get a strong smell. I can't describe the smell; it was not really strong but...'

'It was a sweet smell.'

'Yes, you're right—a very sweet smell.'

'Yes, that was chloroform. Then?'

'The switch was just beside the door. I put on the lights and found that he was sleeping. But I don't know why I became suspicious; the smell was overpowering me. I tried to explain to myself that it was the smell of his medicine, nothing else.

'My legs were shaking, but still I went quietly to his bed. I bent down and saw that he was not breathing. I can't explain what I went through then. I thought I would faint. I think I was losing my balance. To save myself, I clutched on to my uncle's pillow, just next to his neck. Something pricked my hand. I saw a needle which was pierced right into his neck, there was a thread hanging on to the needle.

'I couldn't stand there for another minute. But I don't know how I got away from that room after switching off the lights. When I came to my senses, I found myself shivering and weeping on my own bed.

'You know the rest. I am not suspicious of my brother. I know that he cannot do a thing like this. But I also know that I could not say any of these things to anyone. The next morning, I took a cup of tea to my uncle—although I knew that he was dead.'

Satyabati's voice trailed off. Her pale face and terrified expression told us what she had gone through on that terrible night. I found a strange and excited expression on Byomkesh's face. He said, 'Any other girl would have fainted, become hysterical, screamed and shrieked, but you really are an exceptional girl.'

Satyabati said in a trembling voice, 'I did all that for my brother.'

Byomkesh stood up, 'Now you better go home. I will come to your house tomorrow.'

Satyabati also stood up and said quietly, 'But you haven't said anything.'

Byomkesh said, 'There is nothing to say. I don't want to raise your hopes unnecessarily. There is a person in the middle called Bidhu babu; he may create problems. I can say this much that if you had told me earlier all that you have said today, there would have been no problem.'

With tears in her eyes, Satyabati said, 'I hope my brother won't get into trouble for all that I have said just now. Are you sure? Byomkesh babu, I have no one but my brother in this world.'

Byomkesh got up fast and opened the main door. He tried to smile and said, 'It is quite late. I think you should leave. This is a bachelor's establishment, do you realize?'

Satyabati tried to go out hurriedly. As she passed through the door, Byomkesh said something to her in a low voice. I couldn't hear what he said, but I saw the expression of gratitude on Satyabati's face as she folded her hands in greeting and quickly went down the steps.

'It is half past seven,' Byomkesh said as he sat down after closing the door. 'There is still a lot of time,' he said, doing a bit of mental calculation.

I asked him eagerly, 'Byomkesh! What do you think? I don't see much ray of hope for Sukumar. But from your attitude, I feel that you have realized something.'

Byomkesh shook his head, 'I haven't understood anything as of yet.'

I said, 'Whatever you say. Although all the evidence is pointing against Sukumar, it is my belief that he is not the murderer.'

Byomkesh smiled, 'Then who is the murderer?'

'I don't know that, but it is not Sukumar!'

Byomkesh said nothing. He lifted a cigarette and started smoking. After a long while, he said, 'Satyabati cannot be regarded a beauty—what do you say?'

I was startled, 'Why are you asking that?'

'Just like that. Most people will regard her as a dark-complexioned girl.'

I just couldn't find any link between the present problem and Satyabati's appearance. But I knew that it was very difficult to follow the intricate thought processes of my friend's mind. I gave my considered opinion, 'Yes, most people will find her dark, but not ugly.'

Byomkesh laughed out loud and recited a line from a poem by Tagore about a dark girl. 'Dark? However dark she be, I have seen her dark gazelle-eyes.' Then, turning to me, he asked, 'Ajit, how old are you?'

Stunned, I said, 'My age?'

'Yes, give the correct age—right down to the month and day.'

Maybe the great mystery of Karali babu's death was hidden in the right calculation of my age! Byomkesh was capable of anything unusual. So, I counted the years and months and said, 'I am twenty-nine years, five months and eleven days. But why?'

Byomkesh heaved a sigh of relief and said, 'You are three months older than me, thank God! But please remember this.'

'What do you mean?'

'There is no meaning. Forget it, I am tired of thinking about this case; let's go and watch a film tonight.'

Byomkesh hated going to watch films, so I was very surprised. I said, 'What is wrong with you today? Have you completely lost your mind?'

Byomkesh said, 'Maybe I was born under the sign of the moon. But let's not delay. We'll have our dinner and go out. They are showing a good film at Chitra Cinema Hall.'

After dinner, we went to see the film. It started at about nine-thirty. It was a long film and ended at about a quarter to twelve.

We had to go far; there were still one or two buses plying on the streets. I tried to jump into one. Byomkesh stopped me and said, 'Let's walk for some time,' and started walking very fast.

When he began following a small lane off Cornwallis Street, I realized that he was walking towards Karali babu's house. I couldn't understand what he wanted there at this time of the night. Anyway, I followed him without asking any questions.

We were walking much faster than our normal pace but still, it took quite some time to reach Karali babu's place. There was a street light just next to the main gate of Karali babu's house. Byomkesh stood there and looked at his watch. But it was not necessary to look at the watch, as all the clocks of the city began to strike the midnight hour just then.

Byomkesh thumped my back happily and said, 'It's alright, now let's take a cab and go home.'

∽

The next day, we reached Karali babu's house at about eight-thirty in the morning. Bidhu babu was present there with a few police officials. He looked slightly embarrassed when he saw Byomkesh but quickly covered up the expression by saying gruffly, 'Byomkesh babu, you must have heard that I have arrested Sukumar babu. I knew from the very beginning that he was the culprit. I was just playing a game of cat and mouse with him by keeping him in suspense and hope.'

'Really?' said Byomkesh looking quizzically at Bidhu babu's back, as if in search of the big cat's tail! His junior officers found it hard to conceal their amusement.

Bidhu babu asked suspiciously, 'Why are you here today?'

Byomkesh said, 'Just like that. I heard that another new will has been discovered, so I came to see it.'

Hesitantly and very unwillingly, Bidhu babu pulled out a sheet of paper from his file. 'Be careful,' he said. 'Don't tear it. This is the biggest evidence against Sukumar. After killing Karali babu, Sukumar brought the will to his room and hid it. Do you know where? Have you noticed three trunks in his room, one on top of the other? Well, the will was kept inside the one right at the bottom!'

Byomkesh said with a wide smile, 'Good! Everything is falling in place! But tell me one thing—why didn't Sukumar destroy this will?'

Bidhu babu snorted through his nose, 'Does he have that intelligence? He thought that we would not search his room.'

'Did Sukumar say anything?'

'What will he say? He is doing what every criminal does—pretending to be very surprised and saying that he does not know anything!'

Byomkesh looked at the will, opened the fold with great care and started reading. I began reading the will as well, over his shoulder. It was typewritten on a foolscap page:

I am writing this will on 22 September 1933, in full consciousness and in good health, that after my death, all my money and property will go to my youngest nephew Sri Phanibhusan. All the other wills that were written earlier are hereby being cancelled.

Signed,
Sri Karali

Byomkesh jumped up excitedly. I noticed that his face was flushed with excitement. He said, 'Bidhu babu, the will is so surprising.' Saying this, he gave the paper to Bidhu babu to see.

Bidhu babu read the will thoroughly and said, 'What's the matter? I can't understand...'

'Can't you see?' Byomkesh pointed to the space below the signature.

This time, the wide-eyed Bidhu babu said, 'Oh—witnesses!'

'Quiet!' said Byomkesh, then pointed to the closed door and opened it suddenly.

Makhanlal was eavesdropping; he tried to flee. Byomkesh pulled him into the room by his shirt collar. He pushed Makhan into a chair and said, 'Inspector, keep him here and don't let him speak.' Half-dead with fear, Makhan said, 'I…'

'Quiet! Bidhu babu, get an arrest warrant from the Magistrate. Don't fill in the name of the criminal; we will do that later.' Then he whispered to Bidhu babu, 'In the meantime, try all your tricks with this man. We are going.'

A stunned Bidhu babu said, 'But I can't understand…'

'I will tell you later. But bring the warrant in the meantime. Come, Ajit.'

Byomkesh climbed the stairs with great speed and knocked at Phani's door. Phani opened the door and was surprised to see us.

We entered the room. Byomkesh now seemed relaxed. He said with a broad smile, 'You will be happy to know Phani babu that we have now found out the actual murderer.'

Phani smiled palely and said, 'Yes, Sukumar da has been arrested. But I still can't believe it.'

'It is indeed unbelievable. Another will was found in his room and the beneficiary of that will is none other than yourself.'

Phani said, 'I have heard about that too. I am feeling bitter about the whole affair after I heard the news. For this cursed property, Uncle was murdered.' He heaved a sigh and said, 'Money is the root of all troubles. He has given me all the property, but that doesn't make me happy at all. There was no need for all this. I only wish he was alive.'

Byomkesh stood in front of the bookshelf and said absentmindedly, 'That's true, money is often dearer than sons. What is this book…on physiology? Is it Sukumar babu's?'

Phani said, 'Yes, Sukumar da often lent me his medical

books for reading. It is strange. Through all this, I regarded Sukumar da closer to me than anyone else, even more than my own brothers, and look what he did!'

Byomkesh flipped through the pages of a few other books and said with a note of surprise, 'You are really a bookworm! You have underlined all the books you have read.'

Phani said, 'Yes, I have no other amusement or company other than books. Only Sukumar da used to spend some time with me every evening. Tell me Byomkesh babu, do you really think Sukumar da has committed this crime—is there no doubt at all?'

Byomkesh sat on a chair and said, 'The evidence that we have about the criminal does not leave any scope for doubt. Sit down, I will tell you everything.'

Phani sat on the bed. I sat next to him.

Byomkesh said, 'There are two kinds of murders that are usually committed. One is a crime of passion, when a person kills in a fit of anger. It is easy to catch such a culprit. Most of the time, he confesses on his own. But when a person commits a crime cool-headed, it is very difficult to catch him. It is then that we fail to identify the criminal and begin suspecting others. So, what direction do we follow under such circumstances? Our only way then is to understand the nature of the murderer by the way he has committed the crime.

'In the present case, we noticed something strange—the murderer is clever, and at the same time, foolish. He has committed the murder very intelligently but has left all the evidence in his room like a fool. Just tell me, was there any necessity to kill with Satyabati's needle? Was there no other needle in the market? Again, was there any need to hide the will in a trunk? It could easily be torn and destroyed! So, what conclusion do we draw from this?'

Phani sat thoughtfully with his hand on his chin. 'What conclusion?' he asked after a while.

Byomkesh said, 'A person who is stupid cannot act logically like a clever person. But a person who is clever can act like a stupid person; he can pretend to be foolish. So, it is very clear that the criminal is very intelligent.

'But even a clever person makes mistakes; his attempt to act like a fool sometimes doesn't succeed. In this case as well, the criminal made a few mistakes by which I have been able to catch him.'

Phani said softly, 'What were his mistakes?'

'I will tell you everything, but first…' Byomkesh searched his pocket and took out a plain paper, 'But first, I'll need to make a plan of this house to show you. Can you give me a pencil? Any pencil will do.'

Next to Phani's pillow was a book; he opened it and took out a red pencil from inside it.

Byomkesh looked at the pencil attentively and then with a smile, kept it in his pocket saying, 'There is no need to draw a plan. I'll explain everything to you verbally. The killer of Karali babu made three major mistakes. First, he underlined *Gray's Anatomy* in red. Secondly, he made a slight noise while pulling boxes. Thirdly, he doesn't know the law.'

Phani's face became pale as he whispered, 'Does not know the law?'

Byomkesh said, 'No; that's why this crime of his has not yielded any result.'

Phani licked his dry lips and said, 'I can't understand what you are saying.'

Byomkesh said slowly, 'The will, which was discovered from Sukumar's room, didn't have the signature of witnesses. It is invalid.'

It looked as if Phani would faint that very minute. For a long time, no one said a word. Phani sat staring at the floor. Then suddenly, he pulled at his hair with both hands and said in a violent whisper, 'Useless, useless, everything has been useless. Byomkesh babu, give me some time. I am feeling unwell.'

'I am giving you half an hour, please get ready.' Byomkesh walked to the door and turned, 'You must have thrown the thimble away. Why you did not keep it in Sukumar's room is still a mystery. You had probably forgotten to open it in your haste. Is that correct? But who brought the chloroform for you? Makhan?'

Phani lay on the bed, 'Please come after half an hour,' he said.

We shut the door behind us and came down to the sitting room. Makhan was still sitting between the Inspector and the Sub-Inspector like a zombie. Byomkesh rebuked him with a dark frown, 'When did you buy chloroform for Phani?'

Startled, Makhan said, 'I don't know anything.'

'If you don't speak the truth, we will write the warrant in your name!'

Makhan howled, 'I beg of you, I know nothing. Let me go. Phani told me that he couldn't sleep at night, so if he took a drop of chloroform…so…'

'Alright. Bidhu babu, you can let him go.'

Makhan ran out of the house like the wind! Byomkesh asked, 'Have you got the warrant?'

Bidhu babu said, 'No, it will come right about now. But for whom is the warrant?'

'The warrant is for the person who killed Karali babu.'

Bidhu babu was very annoyed, 'This is no time for jokes, Byomkesh babu! You are favoured by the Commissioner, that's why you are ordering me around and I am bearing with it. But I will not tolerate it if you make fun of me!'

'This is not a joke. It's the truth. Listen to me then…' Byomkesh told Bidhu babu everything in brief. Bidhu babu sat stunned for some time. Then he got up in a hurry, 'If this is true, why did you leave him alone? If he escapes, what will happen then?'

'He will not escape. He will confess to his crimes. That is our only hope. We will not be able to prove his crime in court; the jury will return a verdict of "not guilty" and he will escape!'

'That's true, but…' Bidhu babu sat down again.

We went to Phani's room half an hour later. Bidhu babu walked in front of us, pushed open the door, marched in and stopped short.

Phani was still lying on the bed, his right hand was hanging by the side of his bed, and below it, there was a pool of blood on the floor. Blood was still dripping from the gash on his wrist.

Byomkesh looked at the sight for some time and said, 'I didn't expect this. But what else could he do?'

There was a letter on Phani's chest. Byomkesh picked it up and started reading:

Byomkesh babu,

I am leaving. I am a useless, lame person; no one will need me in this world.

I know that you don't have enough evidence to hang me. But I don't wish to live any longer. For what will I live on if I don't get my uncle's property? What happiness will I have without money?

I am not even a bit sorry for murdering my uncle. He did not love me. He jeered at me because I was lame. I am asking for pardon from Sukumar da. But then, I couldn't have put the blame on anyone else. Besides, with Sukumar da not being there, I would have gained in another way. But it is useless to reveal that innermost secret to anyone now. I will not reveal who brought the chloroform for me because he was not aware of my intentions then. But he was suspicious later.

You are an amazing man; you did not even forget about the thimble! It is true that I forgot to take it out of my finger at that time. It is in this room; you can look for it later. I stole Satyabati's needle and thimble from her sewing box that evening—she was in the kitchen at that time.

I don't think anyone would have been able to catch me, except for you. But even then, I only have admiration and not hate for you.

Yours,
A traveller on a long journey
Phanibhusan Kar

Giving the letter to Bidhu babu, Byomkesh said, 'I don't think there is any problem in releasing Sukumar now. His sister also should be told. I think she is in her room. Come, Ajit.'

∽

A week later, we were having tea in our own sitting room.

For the last few days, Byomkesh was regularly going out in the afternoons. I did not ask why and he told me nothing about his new assignment. I knew that sometimes, he had to deal with very confidential cases about which he was not free to speak—even with me.

I asked, 'Are you going out this afternoon as well?'

He looked at his watch and said, 'Yes.'

I asked hesitantly, 'You are solving a new case, aren't you?'

'Case? Yes, but it is very confidential.'

I did not ask him any questions about it but said, 'Has Sukumar's case been solved?'

'Yes. He has applied for a probate of his uncle's will.'

'Byomkesh, why don't you explain how Phani committed the crime? It is still not clear to me.'

Putting down his cup, Byomkesh said, 'I'll relate the incidents one after the other; listen carefully.'

'That afternoon, there was a quarrel between Karali babu and Motilal. When Sukumar heard about it in the evening, he went to talk to Karali babu. After Sukumar was thrown out of Karali babu's room, he went to Phani's room where he talked to Phani till seven or seven-thirty in the evening. Then, he had his dinner and went to see a film in Chitra Cinema Hall. There is no problem till here.'

'No.'

'Between eight and nine—that is the time when Satyabati was in the kitchen—Phani stole a needle and a thimble from her room. He realized that Karali babu would now change his will again, and this time, it would be his chance to be the beneficiary. He decided that he would not allow the old man to change his mind again. Phani hated the old man. He could not tolerate jeers about his handicap—and Karali babu often did exactly that. I think Phani has been planning to kill him for a long time.

'From the cook's testimony, we know that about half past eleven that night, Motilal went out of the house. Actually, the cook was slightly wrong. Motilal went out at exactly eleven twenty-five at night. It was quite usual for him since he was often not home at night.

'After he went out, Phani came out of his room. Motilal's room is directly below Karali babu's. That is why Phani had to wait till Motilal had gone out, in case there was any noise while he was killing Karali babu. He took about five minutes to chloroform Karali babu; then he pricked his neck with a needle with inexperienced hands. He had to insert the needle three times before he could finally locate the right place. If Sukumar had committed the crime, he would not have made that mistake because he was a medical student.

'After murdering Karali babu, Phani opened his cupboard and found the new will and saw that it was in his name, as he had guessed earlier.

'There was a bit of a doubt here. It could be that Phani first read the will after chloroforming Karali babu and before killing him. Whatever it was, it took him about ten to twelve minutes to complete the whole job.

'Now the question was—what would he do with the will? He could have kept it in the cupboard, but he wanted to implicate Sukumar in the crime. So, he hid the will in the lowest trunk in Sukumar's room. It was necessary for Phani to implicate another person just to save himself from any suspicion.

'He hid the will and the bottle of chloroform in Sukumar's room. He knew that after such a crime, every room of the house would be searched. So the will would eventually be discovered. He would get the property and Sukumar would be hanged.

'Phani made some noise while keeping the will in the trunk, which made Satyabati wake up. It was a quarter to twelve then. She thought her brother had returned from the cinema. But actually, it was impossible for Sukumar to return at that time. He returned when the clocks everywhere struck twelve. Is there anything else to explain?'

'Why was there no signature of witnesses in the will?'

Byomkesh said thoughtfully, 'I think Karali babu wrote the will after dinner. He probably thought that he would ask the cook and the servant to sign the next morning.'

I smoked my cigarette in silence for some time and then asked, 'Did you meet Satyabati later on? What did she say? She must have thanked you profusely?'

Byomkesh said unhappily, 'No, she just touched my feet in silence.'

'I think she is a great girl.'

Byomkesh stood up, pointed a finger at me and said, 'You are older than me. I hope you remember that?'

'Yes, but why?'

Byomkesh entered the next room without answering. When he came out of the room, I found that he had dressed with great care. I said, 'Your secret client seems to have very fine tastes. Did he express his wish to deal with a silk-kurta-clad detective?'

Byomkesh wiped his face with a scented handkerchief and said, 'Yes, it is not easy to seek the truth, is it? It needs a lot of preparation.'

I said sarcastically, 'You have been seeking the truth for a long time, but I have never seen you dress so well.'

Byomkesh said gravely, 'I have started seeking the truth only recently.'

'What does that mean?'

'Have you forgotten a synonym of truth?'

'What?'

'Satya,' saying this, he smiled naughtily and prepared to go out.

'Satya? Oh!' I jumped up and clutched his shoulders, 'Satyabati! I see! So, this is the truth you are seeking these last few days! Oh, Byomkesh! So you have fallen into a trap! The love trap!'

Byomkesh said, 'Be careful, you are older than me, and so you are her elder brother-in-law. So behave like an elder and don't crack jokes. I, too, will call you "dada" from now on!'

I asked, 'Why are you so scared of me?'

Byomkesh said, 'I am suspicious of the entire clan of writers.'

I heaved a sigh and said, 'Alright, I'll be your elder brother—if that's what you want.'

Then I placed the palm of my right hand on Byomkesh's head in mock blessing and said, 'Go, Brother! It is four o'clock. May your mission be successful! I hope that you will always be true to the truth or Satya. I shower my blessings on you.'

Byomkesh went out on this note of good will!

2

The Tantalizing Tarantula
Makorshar Rosh

I literally pushed Byomkesh out the door. For the past month, he has been involved in a very complicated case of forgery. The more intricate the case became, the less he spoke to anyone. Constant peering through documents in his library was affecting his health. If I mentioned this to him, he said, 'Why, I am okay!'

That evening, I said to him, 'I won't listen to you anymore. Let's go for a walk. You should relax for at least two hours a day.'

'But…'

'No buts, let's go for a walk by the lake. Your forger won't run away in these two hours.'

'Alright,' he said ultimately and kept his papers aside; but I knew that his mind was preoccupied with the nameless forger.

While walking along the side of the lake, I met an old friend of mine from college. I had not met him since he took admission in a medical college. I said, 'Hello Mohan, where are you coming from?'

He was pleased to see me, 'Ajit, how are you?'

After the initial joy of the sudden meeting subsided, I introduced him to Byomkesh. Mohan said, 'You are Byomkesh Bakshi? I am so glad to meet you. Sometimes, I used to wonder if the writer of your stories was really my old friend, Ajit Banerjee. But I was never sure.'

I asked, 'What are you doing these days?'

He said, 'I practice in Calcutta.' Then we began strolling together discussing various subjects. After an hour, I noticed that Mohan was eager to say something but was hesitating. Byomkesh too noticed this and asked, 'You have something to say—please go on.'

Mohan said shyly, 'I was thinking of telling you something, but it is such a small thing that I don't want to disturb you unnecessarily.'

I said, 'Please go ahead, if not anything else, you will be rescuing him from the forger.'

'Forger!'

I explained the source of Byomkesh's latest obsession. Mohan said, 'But Byomkesh babu may laugh when I tell him my story.'

Byomkesh said, 'If it is funny, I will, of course, laugh. But looking at your expression, it doesn't seem to be funny. Instead, it seems to me that you are worried about a problem which has been troubling you for some days.'

Mohan said eagerly, 'You are quite right. Perhaps the solution is simple; but for me, it is like a complicated riddle. I am not a fool. In fact, I consider myself moderately intelligent; but a sick, paralytic person is cheating me every single day. You will be surprised to know that I am not the only one. He is making a fool of every member of his family, although they keep a strict vigil on him.'

We sat down on a bench.

Mohan continued, 'I will relate the matter as briefly as possible. I am the family physician at the house of a wealthy person. They have a huge ancestral property. Moreover, they own a market in Calcutta. So you can understand how rich they are.

'The master of this house is Nandadulal babu. He is my patient. He lived such a fast life when he was young that as soon as he turned fifty, his health broke down. He suffers from arthritis and many other ailments. Moreover, he is a paralytic. In our medical jargon, there is a saying that there is nothing unusual about death—what is surprising is how human beings survive! The condition of my patient proves this saying.

'I don't know how I can explain the character of Nandadulal babu. He is foul mouthed, suspicious, jealous and cunning—in one line, I have never met a meaner person than him. He has a wife and sons, but he cannot get along with anyone. He behaves in the same indisciplined manner in which he behaved during his youth. But nature and health are against him. He has no physical strength, so he is angry with the whole world as if everyone is responsible for his condition. He constantly finds an excuse to abuse and harass everyone around him.

'He has no strength and his heart is weak, so he cannot go out of his room. He uses foul language on everyone around and constantly writes on sheafs of paper. His ambition is that he would become a well-known writer one day—so sometimes, he writes in red ink and sometimes in blue. He is furious with publishers and editors because he feels that they don't print his writings out of spite.'

I was curious, 'What does he write?'

'Stories, or you can say some kind of autobiography. Only once did I have a glance at his writing. I could not look at it ever since. After reading it, you feel completely unclean—it is nothing less than pornography. Even the young modern writers of today would have a fit if they read his writing.'

Byomkesh said with a smile, 'I can visualize his character. But what is the problem?'

Mohan gave us two cigarettes and lighted one himself. He said, 'You must be thinking that a person with such qualities may not have any other quirks—you are mistaken. He has a curious quirk that, in spite of his ill health, is addicted to a strange substance.

'Byomkesh babu, you deal with criminals, so you must have seen the basest people addicted to alcohol, marijuana, opium, cocaine, etc., but have you ever heard of anyone addicted to the juice of spiders?'

Mohan puffed at his cigarette excitedly. Startled, I asked, 'What are you saying—spider's juice?'

Mohan said, 'There is a special spider from which this juice is extracted; it is a poisonous drug.'

Byomkesh said to himself, 'Tarantula dance. In Spain, people used to dance uncontrollably after being bitten by this kind of spider. I have read about it in books, but I never knew that it was used in our country.'

Mohan said, 'You are right—a tarantula. It is a common form of addiction in a heterogeneous Spanish tribe of South America. This tarantula juice is actually a dangerous poison; but if taken in small amounts, it provides an excitement to the nervous system. It is a dangerous form of drug addiction. If used regularly, it can cause paralysis of the brain due to the overexcitement of the nerves and consequently result in death.

'Our Nandadulal babu must have gotten addicted to it in his youth. Now even when he is old and infirm, he is unable to give it up. When I became their house physician, he was taking the drug openly—that was about a year back. I stopped it at once saying that if he wished to live, he must give up this addiction.

'There was a tug of war about this issue. He was determined to take it and I was determined to stop him. In the end I said, "I will not allow this stuff to enter your house; let's see how you stop me." He smiled cunningly and said, "Really? I will definitely take the drug. Let's see how you stop it." The battle had begun then.

'All the family members were with me in this, so it was easy to arrange a strong guard in and around the house. His wife and sons were always alert so that the stuff did not reach him. He is virtually immobile, so it was impossible for him to go out and get the drug. I was quite satisfied after making these arrangements with his family.

'But wonder of wonders, in spite of all this strictness, he continued taking the drug. How it was being smuggled to him remained a mystery to everyone.

'At first, I thought that someone in the house was helping him. So, I myself remained in the house guarding him the whole day. You will be surprised to know that he took the drug thrice in front of me, yet I could not make out how. I realized he had taken the drug when I felt his pulse rate, which always doubled with the effect of the drug.

'We searched his room thoroughly and stopped outsiders from visiting him; still we could not stop him. Even now, he is continuing to use the drug.

'Now my problem is how the man gets hold of the spider juice, and if he gets it, how does he take it?'

Mohan fell silent. I don't know if Byomkesh was distracted while listening to him, but as soon as Mohan stopped speaking, he got up and said, 'Ajit, let's go home. I have just thought of something about my case. If I am right, then…!'

I realized that the forger had again brought Byomkesh under his control. It is likely that he did not even listen properly to Mohan. I was a little embarrassed, 'I don't think you heard what Mohan said.'

'Of course I heard! The problem is curious and amusing, but will I have time to solve it? I am occupied with a very serious case.'

Mohan was a little disappointed, 'Never mind—leave it. I

should not have bothered you about such a petty affair. But if you did take some interest, we could have saved a man's life. He may be a horrible human being, but seeing him die slowly with the drug is difficult for a doctor like me to bear.'

Byomkesh was a bit embarrassed, 'I didn't say that I won't take the case. It will also be better to meet the person concerned. But I won't be able to do that today. Rest assured, I will not allow a great man like Nandadulal babu to die. But I will have to return home just now; I think I have solved the case of the forger. I have to look through the papers again. So let Nandadulal babu take the poison to his heart's content tonight. Tomorrow, I will outwit him.'

Mohan smiled, 'Alright, tomorrow I will send the car for you.'

Byomkesh thought for a while and said, 'We can do one thing—let Ajit go with you today. He will come back and give me the details tonight, and I will solve your puzzle either tonight or tomorrow morning.'

I could perceive Mohan's disappointment at my going with him instead of Byomkesh. Byomkesh noticed that too and said, 'Ajit is your old friend. Naturally, familiarity breeds contempt! You don't have much confidence in his powers of detection. But I assure you that my company has sharpened his intelligence! In fact, if I give you a few examples of his great capacity, you will be amazed. Maybe he will solve your mystery himself without my help.'

But Mohan looked unconvinced, even after such high praise. He looked like those anglers who, while expecting huge catches, go home disappointed with small fries. He said, 'Alright, let Ajit accompany me, but if he fails…'

'Then I am there, don't worry,' Byomkesh assured. Then he took me aside and said, 'Observe everything carefully and take note of all the post that comes into the house.' He then left for home.

∽

I had seen Byomkesh solve difficult mysteries. I had also observed and understood his modus operandi by staying with him for the past few years. So I was determined that I would be able to solve this simple problem. I became more determined when Mohan showed his lack of faith in me.

In this frame of mind, I accompanied Mohan and reached our destination in the evening. The streetlights had just been put on. Mohan guided me through a lane off Circular Road. We stopped in front of a big house with an iron gate. It was an old-fashioned house and a gateman was sitting on a stool in front of the gate. Mohan was allowed to enter, but I was stopped. Mohan introduced me as his friend and took me inside.

We crossed the compound and climbed up to the verandah. This time, a young man of twenty or twenty-one approached us. 'Oh doctor? Do come in.' Then he looked questioningly at me and said, 'You are?'

Mohan took him aside and explained my presence. The young man now welcomed me. Mohan now introduced me to the elder son of the owner of the house, Arun. We followed him inside. We passed two rooms and stood in front of the closed door of the third room. As soon as we knocked at the door, we heard a quarrelsome voice from the other side, 'Who...who is disturbing me? Don't bother me, I am writing.'

Arun said, 'Father, the doctor has come. Abhay, open the door.' A young boy of about eighteen opened the door. He was the younger son. We entered the room.

Arun asked Abhay in a whisper, 'Has he taken?' Abhay nodded his head sadly.

The first thing I noticed after entering was a bed in the middle of the room. In that bed, sitting up against the pillows, was a very thin Nandadulal babu with a pen in his hand. He was looking angrily at us. There was a strong light in the room as well as a bedside lamp on a high stool. So I could see the man's face very clearly. He might have been a little under fifty, but his hair was grey. His face was devoid of flesh. His jawbones were sharp enough to pierce his skin. His thin, hooked nose hung on his face. His eyes were unnaturally bright, but without the stimulation of drugs, those very eyes could become dull and lacklustre. His lower lips hung loosely. His overall expression was one of ugly, dissatisfied hunger.

I was surprised looking at this ghost of a man. I noticed that his left hand was jerking upwards, as if it was independent of the rest of his body. This peculiar nervous movement could be compared to the jerks produced in a dead frog with the help of electricity.

Nandadulal babu looked at me angrily and said in a shrill, cracked voice, 'Doctor! Who have you brought in my house? What does he want? Tell him to leave at once, at once!'

Looking at me, Mohan made a sign with his eyes asking me not to mind our host's insulting words. Then he kept aside all the papers strewn on the bed and felt his patient's pulse. Nandadulal babu glanced from me to Mohan with an ugly smile on his face, while his left hand kept jerking up and down. Releasing the man's hand, Mohan asked accusingly, 'So you have taken the drug again?'

'I haven't bought it with your father's money, so what if I have taken the drug—what is it to you?'

Mohan bit his lower lip at the insult and said, 'You are harming yourself. But of course, you won't realize that, you don't have either the capacity or the sense. You are ruining your brain by taking this drug.'

Nandadulal babu made an ugly face and said sneeringly, 'Really? Am I ruining my brain? Then, what about you? You are super intelligent—aren't you? Why can't you catch me then? You have kept guards all around me—but with what result? Hee-hee-hee…' He began to laugh in a derisive shrill and prolonged laughter. It became impossible for Mohan to bear the insult any longer. He got up disgustedly and said, 'It's useless talking to you—do whatever you wish.'

Nandadulal kept on laughing and saying, 'Shame, shame, Doctor…shame, shame! You could not catch me…tee-hee…' He began shaking his thumbs.

I could no longer stand the obnoxious behaviour of this filthy old man—especially in front of his young sons. Mohan, too, lost his patience, 'Please finish your investigation, Ajit, and let us leave this place.'

Suddenly, the man looked at me suspiciously and said, 'But…but, who are you? How dare you enter my house—and with what vile intentions?'

When I did not respond, he continued abusing me, 'Don't act too smart, eh! Don't try your tricks here. Get out of my house right now, otherwise I'll call the police. You are nothing but petty thieves!' He included Mohan in his abuse. Though Nandadulal was not sure why I was there, he was extremely suspicious about my presence.

Arun was embarrassed and whispered to me, 'Don't pay any attention to him. This drug robs him of his senses.'

I began thinking about how terrible this substance was that it so shamefully exposed the ugly subconscious of a human being. How can any sensible and balanced person consume such a poison?

Byomkesh had asked me to observe everything carefully. So

I gave a quick glance around the room. It was big, with very few pieces of furniture in it: one bed, a few chairs, an almirah and a tripod. A lamp was on the table, as well as a bundle of unwritten, plain paper and writing material. Written sheets of paper were scattered on the table. I picked up one sheet and read a few lines—I shuddered with disgust. Mohan was quite right. The contents would indeed have put modern pornographic writers to shame.

Moreover, the most obscene portions were underlined in red ink to attract attention! What a disgusting mind!

I glanced at him with great abhorrence and found that he had gone back to his writing. His Parker pen was moving very fast over the pages. There was another red pen at the side—probably to underline the worst parts. As soon as he completed the page, he took up the red pen and tried it on the page to find that it had dried up. So he dipped it in an ink bottle filled with red ink and concentrated on underlining his 'great piece of literature'.

I turned my face to observe other things in the room. There was nothing in the cupboard except for a few empty bottles of medicine, which Mohan said had been prescribed by him. There were two doors and two windows in the room. We had entered the room through one door, the other led to the bathroom. I peeped into the bathroom too; nothing much there except for some clothes, a towel, soap case, hair oil, toothbrush, etc. The windows did not open outside—in fact, they were seldom opened.

I tried to think along the lines of how Byomkesh would have investigated but could find no clue at all. I was thinking of secret chambers inside the wall when I suddenly noticed that there was a half-finished bottle of some strong Indian perfume on a shelf. I examined it eagerly. There was cotton wool there and also some perfume. 'Does he apply perfume?' I asked his son. He shook his head vaguely and said, 'I don't think so; we don't get any smell.'

'How many days has this bottle been in this room?'

'Always. Father had brought it here.'

I turned round to see that Nandadulal babu was looking in our direction. I was excited. I dabbed a piece of cotton wool in the perfume and put it in my pocket.

Then I looked around the room for the last time and came out. I noticed Nandadulal's eyes following me. He still had that disgusting sneering smile on his face.

We sat in the verandah. I told the family, 'Now I will ask you a few questions. Please don't conceal anything.'

Arun said, 'Please ask.'

'Do you constantly keep an eye on him?'

'Our mother, Abhay and I take turns to be near him. We don't allow any servants to come to him.'

'Have you seen him taking the drug?'

'No, but from his reactions later, we realize that he has taken it.'

'Do you know what it looks like?'

'When he used to take it openly, we saw the drug. It is watery and came in homeopathic bottles. He mixed a few drops in a glass of juice or in some other similar drink.'

'Have you seen that kind of a bottle in his room lately?'

'No, we have searched every corner of his room.'

'Then it must be coming from outside—who brings it?'

Arun shook his head, 'We don't know.'

'Just think carefully. Does no one enter this room except for the three of you?'

'No one, except for the doctor.'

I finished my investigation and wondered what else to do.

I tried to remember Byomkesh's advice and started again, 'Do any letters come to him?'

'No.'

'No parcel or anything like that?'

This time Arun said, 'Yes, a registered letter comes to him every week.'

I jumped up with enthusiasm, 'Where does it come from? Who sends it?'

Arun hung his head in shame and said slowly, 'It comes from this city only, from a woman called Rebecca Lite.'

I asked, 'I understand. Have you read the letters?'

'Yes,' said Arun and looked at Mohan.

I asked eagerly, 'What are the contents of the letters?'

'They are plain sheets of paper.'

'Plain sheets?'

'Yes, only sheets of plain paper are in the envelope. Nothing else.'

I echoed, 'Nothing else?'

'No.'

I was dumbfounded. At last, I said, 'Are you sure there is nothing else in the envelope?'

Arun smiled and said, 'I am sure, because although my father signs and takes the letter, I open it before he does. There's nothing but plain papers.'

'Do you always open the letter? Where do you open it?'

'In my father's room—the postman delivers the letter in his room, in my presence. My father is an invalid and cannot move.'

'But this is very strange. What's the meaning of sending plain paper by registered post?'

Arun was silent, then shook his head and said, 'I don't know.'

I sat for some time, feeling like a fool. Then I heaved a sigh and got up. I was hopeful when I had heard about the registered letter—but, no—there is no ray of hope on that end. I realized that the case was not as simple as it apparently seemed to be and that my intelligence will not be enough to solve the case. The lecherous old and invalid drug addict would make a fool of me. Byomkesh, with his incisive perception, was needed to solve this strange case.

Crestfallen, I said that I would relate every detail to Byomkesh. Suddenly, I remembered something, 'Does Nandadulal babu write to anyone?'

Arun said, 'No, but he sends a money order every month.'

'To whom?'

Shamefacedly he said, 'To that Jewish woman.'

Mohan elaborated, 'In the past, that woman was Nandadulal babu's...'

'I understand. How much does he send?'

'A hundred, but we don't know why he sends the money.'

I thought to myself—pension—but said nothing. I went home alone while Mohan stayed back.

ᔥ

I reached home at eight in the night. Byomkesh was in the library. As soon as I knocked, he opened the door and asked, 'What news? Have you solved the problem?'

'No,' as I sank into a chair. Byomkesh was reading through the documents with a magnifying glass. He looked at me sharply, 'What's wrong with you? Since when have you started using perfume—like a fop?'

'No, no... I have brought it for you.'

I explained everything in detail. In the end, I said, 'I have failed brother; see if you can do anything. I feel you might get some clue if you analyze the perfumed cotton wool.'

'What will we get—spider juice?' He took the cotton wool

from me and inhaled it, 'Ah! Very good and expensive perfume. What did you say? If we analyze it, what will we get?'

More hesitant than before, I mumbled, 'Maybe Nandadulal babu is taking the drug under the pretence of applying the perfume.'

Byomkesh burst into laughter, 'How can you hide anything which has such a strong smell? Did you get any proof that Nandadulal uses perfume?'

'No, I didn't...but...'

'No... No use investigating from that angle. Try another angle. How does the drug come into his room, and how does he put it into his mouth, in spite of such strict vigilance? Think along those lines. Who sends plain paper in registered post and why? Why is money sent to the woman—have you thought about all this?'

I said despairingly, 'I have thought a lot... I don't think I can do anything. It's not my cup of tea.'

'Think again—where there is a will, there is a way. Think deeply, concentrate and don't give up.' Saying this, he picked up the magnifying glass.

'What about you?' I asked.

'I am thinking too, but I cannot concentrate—my forger...' He peered into his papers.

I sat on the easy chair in our sitting room and started thinking again. Really, why should I not succeed? Of course, I will.

Firstly, why are sheaves of plain paper sent by registered post? Is something written there with invisible ink? How does that benefit Nandadulal babu? The papers do not reach him directly. Even if we take it for granted that the drug does reach him somehow, is it possible to hide the bottles in which it comes from the strict scrutiny of his family members? Then, what is the answer?

I was so excited while thinking about this problem that I smoked about five cigarettes at a stretch and still had no clue whatsoever. I was about to throw up my hands in dismay, when an idea struck me all of a sudden! I sat up in my chair.

Is it possible? Why not? It does sound a little weird, but everything is possible in a case, according to Byomkesh, even if it seems impossible in the beginning. I felt that this was the only solution.

As I was getting up to talk to Byomkesh, he himself came out of the room.

'Have you thought of a solution?' He asked.

'I think so.'

'Good! What is your solution?'

I felt a little awkward about telling him my idea, but still I said, 'I saw quite a few spiders on the walls of Nandadulal babu's room. I feel that he is...'

'Catching them and eating them up?' Byomkesh laughed out loud, 'Ajit, you are incomparable—you are a genius. If he ate up the spiders in his room, he would not get the kick but die of poisoning. There would be sores and boils all over his body.'

I was very annoyed, 'So what is the solution—you tell me.'

He sat on a chair and lifted his feet on a low table. He began smoking a cigar idly and asked, 'Did you understand why the plain sheets arrive by registered post?'

'No.'

'Why was money sent to the woman? Why Nandadulal babu writes obscene stories?'

'No, have you understood?'

'I think so,' Byomkesh said with half closed eyes. 'But first, I have to clear my doubts about something—only then can I give a definite answer.'

'About what?'

Byomkesh closed his eyes and said, 'I must know the colour of Nandadulal babu's tongue.'

I got even angrier thinking that Byomkesh was making fun of me, 'So you are joking now?'

'Joking?' He opened his eyes and said, 'Are you angry? But I am serious. Everything depends now on the colour of his tongue. If it is bright red, then I will know that my assumption is correct. And if it isn't... Did you notice it?'

I said angrily, 'No, I didn't have the time to note the colour of his tongue.'

'But that was the first thing you should have noticed. Anyway, ring up his son and find out.'

'I hope he won't think that I am pulling his leg?'

Byomkesh said dramatically, 'Fear not, fear not, my dear friend!'

I went to the next room and rang up the number. Mohan was still there. He said, 'I didn't think it was necessary, so I did not mention it. Nandadulal babu's tongue is bright red. It is a bit unnatural because he does not eat paan. Why are you asking this?'

I called Byomkesh and he said to Mohan, 'The riddle is solved! It was Ajit who solved the mystery. I helped him a bit only. I was busy with my forger... Yes, I have caught him. You don't have to do much. Just remove the red ink bottle and red pen from his room. Yes, you are right. Please come tomorrow; I will tell you everything then. Yes, I will thank Ajit on your behalf. Didn't I tell you that his intelligence has heightened these days?' Byomkesh hung up the phone laughing.

After coming back to the sitting room, I said shyly, 'I think I have understood it a little. But you must tell me everything clearly. How did you understand?'

Byomkesh looked at the clock and said, 'Putiram will call us for dinner any moment now. Alright, I will tell you everything in a nutshell. First of all, you should have investigated how the drug was being brought into the room. It can't walk into the room by itself—so someone must be bringing it. Since Nandadulal is an invalid, who could it be? Five people are allowed to enter the room—the doctor, the wife, the two sons and the postman. The first four will not give him the drug—so it must be the postman. So the drug must be coming in through him.'

'But there was nothing in the envelope except plain paper.'

'That was the red herring that fooled everyone. It was expected that the drug would be in the envelope, so no one noticed the postman. This man was very cunning—he took advantage of the situation. While the son was busy signing the paper to receive the registered letter, the postman quickly exchanged the red ink bottle. He was paid to do so. The only reason to send the envelope with plain paper was to allow the postman to enter the room.'

'Then?'

'You made another mistake. The money sent to the woman was not her pension. Giving pension to an ex-mistress is an unheard-of thing. It was the price of the drug—the woman was the supplier of the drug.'

'Well, the drug reached Nandadulal babu, but how did he take it with all eyes riveted on him?'

'So Nandadulal started writing stories. All the writing materials are near his bed. He writes with his blue pen and underlines with the red pen and sucks the nib of the pen whenever he gets a chance. Now do you understand why the colour of his tongue is red?

'The drug is very expensive. He was using more of the blue ink and much less of the red. He could not afford to waste the drug and used it sparingly in the red ink.'

'It is so easy!' I sighed.

'It is easy, but because it was easy, no one could catch the man. He is a sharp-witted old fellow.'

'How did you solve it?'

'Very simple. Two things seemed totally redundant. Firstly, the sending of blank paper, and secondly, the man's writing habit. As soon as I started investigating the real reason behind these apparently useless actions, I unearthed the truth.'

The telephone rang in the next room. Byomkesh spoke into the phone, 'Doctor, what's wrong? Nandadulal babu is screaming and throwing a tantrum? Let him be and just ignore his abuses. He is bad-mouthing Ajit? I don't think he minds... Ajit knows that it is difficult to get praised for everything in life. Every good deed is accompanied with some snag—like the sting of a bee in its honey, like the beauty of the rose with its thorns. That's the way of the world. Goodbye!'

3

A Thorn in the Flesh
Ponther Kanta

Byomkesh folded the newspaper neatly, took a look out the window and got relaxed in a chair. The clear February sky was bright with sunlight.

We occupied a few rooms in the second floor of the house. From the window, a part of the city as well as a part of the sky could be seen clearly. If one looked below, one could see the busy traffic on Harrison Road. This hurry and scurry could be observed in the sky too. A host of sparrows was flying busily around, and above them a flight of doves seemed to be flying higher and higher as if to encircle the sun.

It was eight in the morning. We had finished our breakfast and were reading newspapers to get acquainted with the ways of the world.

Byomkesh looked away from the window and said, 'For the last few days, a strange advertisement has been appearing in the newspaper. Did you notice it?'

I said, 'No, I don't see or read advertisements.'

Byomkesh lifted his eyebrows in surprise and said, 'You don't read advertisements? Then what do you read?'

I said, 'What everyone reads—the news!'

'That means rubbish, news like who has cut a finger in Manchuria...or who had a triplet in Brazil! What's the use of reading all that? If you want to get real news, read advertisements.'

Byomkesh is a strange man. Looking at him, one would never realize that there was something great in him. But if you tease him, disagree with him and excite him, then a different person emerges from within him—like a tortoise emerging from its shell. He is a reserved person, but if anyone makes him angry by mocking him, then whatever he says is really worth listening to. So, I couldn't resist the temptation of poking him. 'Oh really? Then these newspaper owners are very wicked people. Instead of filling their papers with advertisements, they even give useless news?'

Byomkesh's eyes became sharp, 'It is not their fault. If they don't cater to people like you, there will be no sale of the newspapers. So, they have to create news. But the real news is in the advertisements. What is happening throughout the country, who are involved in daylight robbery and who are planning to smuggle contraband—these kinds of useful news are found in advertisements. You don't find it in Reuters.'

I laughed and said, 'That's true, but…never mind…from now on, I will only read advertisements. But which funny advertisement were you talking about?'

Byomkesh passed the paper to me and said, 'Read. I have underlined it.'

While turning the pages, I noticed a small, three-line advertisement in one corner, underlined in red. Since it was underlined, I noticed it, or else it would have been difficult to find.

THORN IN THE FLESH

If anyone wants to get rid of a thorn in the flesh, then on a Saturday at five-thirty in the evening, stand with your hand resting on the lamp post on the southwest corner of the 'White Way Ladle Shop.'

I read the advertisement twice or thrice but could not make any head or tail of it. Amazed, I asked, 'If I stand resting my hand on a lamp post, I'll get rid of the thorn in my flesh! What is the meaning of this advertisement, and what is the meaning of a thorn in the flesh?'

Byomkesh said, 'That I have not discovered as yet. This advertisement is being published every Friday for the last three months now. If you look through the old newspapers, you will find out.'

I said, 'But what is the meaning of this advertisement? Advertisements are given with a purpose. This one does not seem to have any meaning at all.'

Byomkesh said, 'Right now, it does not seem to make any sense; but that may not be true. No one spends money to advertise needlessly. One thing becomes clear if you read it.'

I asked, 'What?'

'The person who has put in this advertisement does not wish to reveal his identity. Firstly, there are no names in the advertisement. The names of advertisers are not given at times, but the box number is always given. However, there is nothing like that here. Whoever puts in an advertisement wishes to do business with the public—this advertisement is no exception to that. But the strangest thing is that he doesn't wish to disclose his identity but wishes to work behind the scenes.'

'I don't understand.'

'Alright, the advertiser wants to tell the public—those who wish to get rid of the thorn in the flesh, stand at such and such place at a certain time so that I can recognize you. We won't go into a debate on the thorn in the flesh. Now let us assume that you want to make contact with the person. What do you do? You go and stand at the appointed place with your hand on the lamp post... Then what happens?'

'What happens?'

'Can you imagine the crowd in that area at five-thirty on a Saturday evening? On one side, you have the huge departmental store, on the other is New Market, and then there are four or five cinema houses surrounding the area. You are standing there and being pushed by the moving crowd. But nothing happens... Your wish is not granted. You get impatient and go away thinking that the whole thing was a hoax, a practical joke. Suddenly, you find a letter in your pocket... You have no idea who has put it in your pocket in that surging crowd.'

'Then?'

'Then what! The thief doesn't meet the ironsmith but the duplicate key has been ordered! A connection is established between you and the advertiser, but you know nothing about how he looks or who he is.'

I kept quiet for some time and then asked, 'If your assumption is correct, then what does it prove?'

'It proves that the person wants to keep his identity a secret, and a person who is so careful about this may be a person full of humility, but he is not a good soul.'

I said, 'This is only your conjecture—you can prove nothing.'

Byomkesh said, 'But conjecture leads to real proof. There is a thing called 'circumstantial evidence' in the court of law. What are these, except conjectures? On the basis of these conjectures, people are being sent to life imprisonment.'

I kept quiet. I couldn't quite agree with Byomkesh that conjecture could be used as evidence. But it was difficult to disagree with Byomkesh's point of view. So I decided to keep quiet. I knew that my silence would irritate him, and he would put forth a more forceful argument.

A small sparrow was sitting above our window with a bit of straw, looking around.

Byomkesh stood up, pointed at the bird and said, 'What does the bird want?'

I said, 'The bird? Must be looking for a place to build its nest.'

'Are you sure? You have no doubt?'

'No, I have no doubt.'

Byomkesh smiled and said, 'How did you know? Where is the proof?'

'Proof? It's carrying a straw on its beak!'

'Just because it is carrying a piece of straw, it proves that the bird is looking to build a nest?'

I knew I was trapped.

'Conjecture—now do you agree? Why were you arguing all this time?'

'But do you mean to say that whatever is true of a sparrow will be true of a human being?'

'Why not?'

'If you sit on a window with a piece of straw in your mouth, what will it prove? That you want to build a house?'

'No, it will prove that I am mad.'

'Is there any need to prove that?'

Byomkesh began laughing, 'You can tease me but you can't make me angry, and you have to agree to what I have been saying—a logical conjecture is as good as visible evidence.'

I said stubbornly, 'But whatever you said about that advertisement is too far-fetched—I cannot believe it.'

'That's your weakness... It is better to give visible evidence to a person like you. Tomorrow is Saturday and we don't have much to do... I will give you your proof tomorrow.'

'But how?'

There were sounds of footsteps on our staircase. Byomkesh was all ears.

'An unknown person…heavily built…even plump…has a walking stick. He must have come to meet us, as we are the only residents on this floor,' Byomkesh smiled.

There was a knock on the door. Byomkesh said, 'Come in, please. The door is open.'

The gentleman who came in was an elderly, plump gentleman with a silver-handle walking stick. He wore a black, high-necked coat and dhoti. He was fair, clean-shaven and bald. He was panting after climbing the stairs. So, he could not speak for some time. He took out a handkerchief and began wiping his face.

Byomkesh whispered to me, 'Conjecture, conjecture!'

I swallowed his ridicule silently. It was true that his description exactly fitted the stranger.

The gentleman took a breath and said, 'Who is detective Byomkesh babu?'

Byomkesh switched on the fan, pointed to a chair and said, 'Sit down, please. My name is Byomkesh Bakshi, but I don't like the word detective—I am a truth seeker. Whatever it is, you seem very agitated. Cool down and tell me about the mystery of the gramophone pin.'

The gentleman sat on a chair and stared at him in amazement. I was surprised as well. How Byomkesh could associate this elderly gentleman with the gramophone pin mystery was beyond my comprehension. I had seen many aspects of his great talent, but this seemed to me like magic.

The gentleman controlled himself with great difficulty and said, 'You…you... How did you know?'

With a big smile, Byomkesh said, 'It is only a conjecture! Firstly, you are elderly; secondly, you are well off; thirdly, you are in great trouble; and lastly, you need my help. So…'

His incomplete sentence and expression showed that the rest was simple enough for a child to realize.

It is better to relate here that for the past few days, a strange and mysterious thing has been happening in Calcutta. All the vernacular and English dailies were calling it the 'Gramophone Pin Mystery', and creating a lot of noise all around. As a result, the people of Calcutta were curious, excited and terrified. It was the hot topic of discussion in tea shops and everyone was frightened about stepping out their doors.

About a month or half back, Joyhari Sanyal of Sukia Street was walking along Cornwallis Street in the morning. As soon as he stepped down from the pavement to the street, he fell on his face. There were a lot of people around who carried him away from the street, but found that he was dead. After investigation, it was found that there was no sign of any injury except for a drop of blood on his chest. The police sent the body to the hospital suspecting it to be an accident. After the post mortem, it was found that the reason for his death was a gramophone pin that had pierced his heart. This pin must have been shot with something like a gun directly into the chest of the victim. It pierced the skin and flesh and struck the heart, resulting in instant death.

There was a lot of stir in the newspapers regarding this death, and a short biography of the man was also published. Was it murder? If it was, then how was it committed? There were lots of debates on it. Things were not clear. Why was the crime committed, and what was the motive behind the murder? The police were still investigating. The bigwigs at the tea shops declared that it was nothing but a case of a massive heart attack. The newspapers were starved of good news items, so they were fabricating interesting stories.

About eight days later, the news that came out was a source

of great excitement for the middle-class Bengali society. The wise men at the tea shops were wide-eyed with wonder. Rumours and stories began sprouting like mushrooms during the monsoon.

The *Daily Kalketu* wrote:

AGAIN A GRAMOPHONE PIN
A Strange Thrilling Mystery

The streets are not safe in Calcutta. The readers of Kalketu are aware that a few days back, Joyhari Sanyal died while he was walking on the road. As stated by the doctors, the cause of his death was a gramophone pin. We were sure that it was no ordinary incident, and there was a terrible secret hidden in the whole affair. We have been proven right. There occured a similar incident yesterday as terrible as the first. Kailash Chandra Moulik, one of Calcutta's famous rich, was going on a drive at about five-thirty in the evening at the Maidan. Near Red Road, he stopped the car and got down to take a walk. After he had walked a short distance, he fell to the ground. His driver and a few others brought him to the car. He was dead. Everyone was stunned by the suddenness of the incident, but fortunately, the police arrived fast. Kailash babu was wearing a silk kurta. The police found a drop of blood on his chest. Suspecting an accident, his body was sent immediately to a hospital. According to the post-mortem report, a gramophone pin was stuck in his heart. This pin was shot at him from the front.

It is obvious that this is not a sudden accident. A group of heinous murderers is roaming the streets of Calcutta. It is difficult to fathom who they are and why they are killing the elite of the city. The strangest thing is the method in which they are being killed. With what weapon and from where they are committing these murders remains a mystery.

Kailash babu was a kind-hearted and gentle person. It was not possible for him to have any enemies. When he died, he was only forty-eight years old. He was a widower and had no sons. His only daughter was the heir to the property. We convey our sympathies to his daughter and son-in-law. The police are investigating, and they have arrested his driver, Kali Singh.

There was uproar in the newspapers for the next fortnight. The police increased the tempo of their investigation and probably exhausted their efforts as no ray of light could be shed on the mystery. Any arrest of the culprits was a far cry.

The gramophone pin appeared again after a gap of fifteen days. Its target now was a wealthy businessman of the goldsmith clan—Krishnadayal Lana. He was walking across the Dharmatala and Wellington Street crossing when he too fell and did not get up. The newspapers began buzzing again. The inefficiency of the police was criticized bitterly. The citizens of Calcutta moved around with great fear in their hearts. This became the hot topic of discussion everywhere. After this, there were two other similar deaths in quick succession. The city was paralysed with fear and could find no means of defending itself.

Needless to say, Byomkesh was deeply interested in this mystery. His job was to catch thieves and criminals, and he had already earned a good reputation. Although averse to the nomenclature of a 'detective', he knew that he was nothing but one. So the strange murders excited his mind. We had visited the spots where these crimes had taken place. Byomkesh may have gathered some clues while doing so, but I was unaware of it. Whatever news he received about the gramophone pin mystery was noted down with great care in his notebook. He probably hoped that one day, he would be able to lay his hands on some clinching, ultimate clue to this mystery.

So now, when a clue had come right into his hands, he seemed excited and impatient; although outwardly, he looked cool and calm.

The gentleman said, 'I had heard your name…now I find that I have come to the right place. The proof of your great ability makes me certain that you will be able to save me from this great danger. The police have not been able to do anything—I haven't even gone to them. Five murders have been committed, and they have not been able to solve anything. I would have been dead as well!'

His voice became tremulous and began to perspire profusely.

Byomkesh comforted him, 'Don't be upset. It's good that you have come to me instead of going to the police. Now tell me everything from the beginning. Don't leave out anything even if you think it is not important. There is nothing unimportant to me.'

The gentleman controlled himself and said, 'My name is Ashutosh Mitra. I stay in Nebutala. From the age of eighteen, I have been travelling for my business. I haven't had time even to marry and settle down. Besides, I don't like the burden of children. So I did not even feel like getting married. I am a neat person and I like to stay alone. I am not young either—I will be fifty-one next January. I retired from work about two years back. I have invested a good amount of money in the bank, and I can manage very well with the interest. I don't have to pay rent as the house is my own. I like music, and I am spending my days quite happily pursuing this hobby.'

Byomkesh asked, 'Do you have a dependent?'

'No, I have no relatives, so I don't have these problems. Yes, I do have a good-for-nothing nephew who used to bother me for money, but the fellow is a drunkard and a gambler. I can't tolerate those types of people, so I don't allow him to come to my house anymore.'

Byomkesh asked, 'Where does your nephew stay?'

Ashu babu said with great satisfaction, 'Right now, in jail. He fought with the police in an inebriated state and was thrown into jail for two months.'

'Please continue.'

'With Binod in jail, I had a very peaceful time. I have no friends. But I have done no harm to anyone—so I did not think I had any enemies. However, yesterday there was a bolt from the blue. I just couldn't imagine that such a thing could happen. I had read about the gramophone pin mystery, but I didn't believe it. I thought that it was all a cock and bull story. But now, I know that I was mistaken.

'Last evening, I went out as usual. Every evening, I go to a musical soirée in Jorasanko. I spend the evening there and come back home by nine or nine-thirty at night. I walk the distance—it is a good exercise for me at my age. Last night, as I was returning home, I had reached the Amherst Street and Harrison Road crossing at exactly a quarter past nine. There was still a lot of traffic in the street. I waited on the pavement to cross the road. Two trams went by and then I tried to cross. When I reached the middle of the street, I felt a tremendous blow on my chest. I felt a pinprick on the skin near my chest. I felt as if someone had punched me hard on my pocket watch. I nearly toppled over but somehow managed to keep my balance and crossed over to the pavement. I was quite confused. I couldn't understand how I had received the blow on my chest. I tried to pull out the watch from my breast pocket but found that it was stuck. When I carefully pulled out the watch, I found that its glass cover was completely shattered and…and…a gramophone pin had pierced the watch.'

He began perspiring again and pulled out a small box with a watch with trembling hands. Byomkesh opened the box and took out the watch. It had no glass cover and had stopped exactly at nine-twenty. In its centre was stuck a gramophone pin. It had pierced the watch through and through and was peeping out viciously from the back of the watch. Byomkesh kept the watch back in the box and asked, 'Then?'

Ashu babu said, 'I don't remember how I returned home. I couldn't sleep a wink because of anxiety and fear. Thank God I had the pocket watch! It saved my life, or else I would have been in the morgue as well.' He shivered, 'I have aged ten years overnight. Throughout the night, I kept thinking about where I should escape and how I will save my own life… In the end, I remembered you. I had heard about your great talents…so I have come running to you. I came in a closed car. I didn't dare to walk…in case…'

Byomkesh got up and placed a hand on Ashu babu's shoulder, 'Rest assured, you have nothing to fear. There was indeed a great risk to your life yesterday. But if you listen to my instructions, you have nothing to fear in the future.'

Ashu babu clasped Byomkesh's hands and said, 'If you save me Byomkesh babu, I will give you a reward of a thousand rupees.'

Byomkesh sat on his chair and smiled, 'That's good! The government has declared a reward of two thousand; with yours, it makes three. But first, answer a few of my questions. Yesterday, when you felt that blow on your chest, did you hear any sound?'

'What kind of sound?'

'Something like a tyre burst?'

Ashu babu said positively, 'No.'

'Any other sound?'

'I cannot remember anything else.'

'Think hard.'

After thinking for some time, Ashu babu said, 'I heard traffic moving on the street... Come to think of it, when I felt the blow, I heard the ring of a bicycle bell.'

'You did not hear any unnatural sound?'

'No.'

After remaining silent for some time, Byomkesh asked, 'Do you have any enemy who would like to murder you?'

'No. At least none that I know of.'

'You are not married, so you have no children. Your nephew must be your heir?'

He hesitated a little and said, 'No.'

'Have you made your will?'

'Yes.'

'Who is the beneficiary to your will?'

Ashu babu blushed with embarrassment; he kept quiet for some time and said hesitantly, 'You can ask me every other question but this. It is a very private and personal affair.'

Byomkesh looked at him sharply and said, 'Leave it. Does the person who is your heir know about your will?'

'No, only my lawyer and I know about it.'

'Do you meet your heir?'

'Yes,' said Ashu babu, looking askance.

'How long has your nephew been in jail?'

Ashu babu thought for some time and said, 'About three weeks.'

Byomkesh sat thinking for some time. Then taking a deep breath, he stood up, 'You leave your address and your watch. If I need to know anything more, I will contact you.'

Ashu babu said anxiously, 'But you have not done anything for me yet... What if I am attacked again?'

Byomkesh said, 'All you have to do is to remain at home—try not to go out.'

Ashu babu said with a pale face, 'I stay alone in the house, if…'

Byomkesh said, 'No, there is no danger inside the house, you can rest assured. But if you want to keep a watchman, you could.'

Ashu babu asked, 'Will I not be able to go out at all?'

Byomkesh thought for sometime and said, 'If you have to go out, walk on the pavement—but beware! Don't walk on the streets. If you do, I won't be able to guarantee the continuance of your life.'

After Ashu babu left, Byomkesh sat down with a frown, no doubt thinking over all the new clues that he got. I did not disturb him by asking any questions. He opened his mouth half an hour later. 'You must be thinking why I asked Ashu babu not to walk on the streets and how I guessed that he is safe at home.'

'Yes,' I said.

Byomkesh said, 'You must have noticed something about the gramophone pin—all the murders were committed in the middle of the street. Did you wonder why this was happening?'

'No, what's the reason?'

'There are two reasons: firstly, it is impossible to catch the culprit if he commits the murder in the middle of a busy street; secondly, the weapon with which these murders are committed can be used only in the middle of a street.'

'What kind of a weapon is that?'

Byomkesh said, 'When I get to know that, the mystery of the gramophone pin will be solved.'

I was struck with an idea, 'A person may have invented a special kind of gun from which gramophone pins can be shot.'

Byomkesh looked at me admiringly, 'You have really used your brain! But there are a few problems about that. A person who wants to kill with a pistol or a gun will not choose the middle of the street to commit the crime; he will rather look for a quiet, secluded place. Leave alone a gun, even the sound of a pistol cannot be muffled by the noise of the traffic. Besides that, what about the smell of gunpowder? Sound may cover up sound, but what about the smell?'

I said, 'What if they use an airgun?'

Byomkesh laughed, 'To carry an airgun to commit a murder is indeed a novel idea, but not a very practical one. No, no…it is not so easy… The one thing to think about is that whatever weapon is being used, there has to be a sound. How has that sound been concealed?'

I told him, 'You just said that sound covers up sound.'

Suddenly, Byomkesh sat up straight, stared wide-eyed at me and said in a hushed voice, 'That's right, that's right!'

I was surprised at his reaction and said, 'What happened?'

Byomkesh shook off his thoughts and said, 'Nothing. The more one thinks about the gramophone pin mystery, the more one comes to the conclusion that all these murders are connected to each other; every single one of them has a similarity—which is not always apparent.'

'How?'

Byomkesh counted off on his fingers, 'Firstly, those who have been murdered are not young. Even Ashu babu, who escaped because of his pocket watch—they are all elderly; secondly, they are all wealthy; thirdly, all of the victims were murdered in the middle of different streets in front of hundreds of people; and lastly—and this is the most important fact—none of them had sons.'

I said, 'So you surmise that…'

Byomkesh said, 'I don't surmise anything. These are my conjectures or premises.'

I said, 'But it is difficult to catch the culprits depending on conjectures and premises.'

Byomkesh said, 'Not culprits, but culprit. Even though the newspapers are screaming about a gang of murderers, there is but one in the gang; he is the one and only man responsible for planning and executing these crimes.'

I asked doubtfully, 'How can you be so sure? Do you have any proof?'

Byomkesh said, 'There are many proofs. But right now, one is sufficient to prove my point. Is it possible for more than one person to have a perfect aim? Every pin found its mark exactly into the heart of each victim. Ashu babu was saved by his pocket watch, or else the pin would have reached its target. It is like the legendary aim of Arjuna to win Draupadi in the Mahabharata. How many Arjunas were there? Only one, even in those days of great heroism.' He got up laughing.

Next to the sitting room, there was another room. It was Byomkesh's personal room. Even I was not allowed there all the time. In reality, this room was his library, laboratory, museum and green room. Picking up Ashu babu's watch, he entered the room saying, 'I will investigate the mystery of this watch after lunch. Now let me take a shower; it's getting late.'

∽

At about three in the afternoon, Byomkesh went out. I did not know why he had gone out. He returned in the evening. I was waiting for him when tea was served. We drank our tea in silence; having tea together had become a habit with us.

Later, Byomkesh relaxed in a chair with a cheroot and asked, 'What kind of man is Ashu babu, in your opinion?'

I was a little surprised, 'Why? I thought he was a nice and simple man.'

Byomkesh said, 'And his character?'

I said, 'He dislikes his drunken nephew so much that it seems to me that his character is okay. Besides, he is an elderly man, and he is not married. He could have had some escapades in his younger days—but now he is too old.'

Byomkesh smiled meaningfully and said, 'He may be too old, but a woman is involved, nevertheless. The musical soirée to which he goes every evening in Jorasanko is at that lady's house. I should not say that it is her house because Ashu babu pays the rent, and it is not a musical soirée as it involves only two people—Ashu babu and that lady.'

'What can you say? The old man is young at heart!'

'Not only that, but for the last ten to twelve years, Ashu babu has managed the upkeep of this lady. You must admit that he is devoted to her. Even the other party is very devoted as no other music lover is allowed in her house; there is strict vigil at the door.'

I was interested, 'Really? Did you go there disguised as a music lover? Did you see her? What does she look like?'

Byomkesh said, 'I saw her for a second. I don't want to disturb the mental balance of a bachelor like you by describing her beauty. In one word, she is stunning—aged twenty-six or twenty-seven—but she looks about nineteen or twenty. One has to give credit to Ashu babu's taste in women.'

I laughed and said, 'I can see that. But why are you so interested in Ashu babu's private life?'

Byomkesh said, 'Unlimited curiosity is my weakness. Besides, I was a little doubtful about the beneficiary to Ashu babu's will.'

'So she is Ashu babu's heiress?'

'That's what I think. I met another gentleman there—a

well-dressed young man of about thirty-five or thirty-six—who quickly pressed a letter into the hands of the watchman and disappeared fast. But leave it, this fact is interesting but of no use to me.'

He stood up and began pacing the floor. I realized that he didn't wish to get distracted by trivialities like Ashu babu's private life. His present responsibility was to save Ashu babu from danger. Realizing that we often get misguided by unimportant details and forget important issues, I said, 'Did you get any clues from the watch?'

Byomkesh stood in front of me and said smilingly, 'I learnt three facts from the watch. Firstly, I realized that when the pin was shot, the distance between the victim and the murderer was about seven or eight yards—because the gramophone pin is so light that it would not find its mark at a distance greater than that. But you must have seen how accurate the aim of the murderer was each time he killed his prey.'

I said with amazement, 'It was shot at a distance of only seven or eight yards, yet no one caught the murderer?'

Byomkesh said, 'That is the greatest mystery of all. Just think, after the murder, the murderer was somewhere near, among the spectators. He may even have helped to carry the dead body to the hospital, and yet no one realized it! How did he ever do that?'

I thought for some time and said, 'It could be that the murderer carries a weapon in his pocket that is suitable for shooting gramophone pins. He comes near his prey and fires that weapon from inside his pocket; and since there are men who walk with their hands in their pockets, no one would be suspicious.'

Byomkesh said, 'If that was the case, then he could have done his job on the pavement. Why did he have to get down on the street? Besides, I don't know of any weapon which can shoot so silently and pierce the heart of a human being. Do you realize the amount of strength and power that is required for that?'

I kept quiet. Byomkesh sat thinking for a long time with his hands on his chin; then he said, 'I feel there is a very simple solution to this, but I am not being able to grasp it. The solution eludes me as soon as I am about to grasp it.'

We did not discuss this business that evening. Even before going to bed, Byomkesh remained distracted. His mind was following the solution like an arrow follows its prey. I didn't disturb him.

༄

The next morning, he got up from bed with a worried expression. He quickly had a cup of tea, and went out. He came back after about three hours. When I asked him where he had gone, he said vaguely, 'To the lawyer's house.' When I found him distracted, I didn't disturb him further.

He looked happier later that afternoon. He had been walking in his room behind closed doors. Once, I heard him speak on the phone. About four-thirty in the afternoon, he stuck his neck out of his room and said, 'Have you forgotten what we had decided yesterday? We were going to get definite proof for "Thorn in the Flesh".'

It was true, I had completely forgotten about 'Thorn in the Flesh'. Byomkesh said smilingly, 'Come, let me dress you up a bit.'

He opened a cupboard and took out a tin box. From it, he took out a pair of scissors, spirit-gum, crepe and a variety of items. While putting spirit-gum with a brush, he said, 'Many criminals know that Ajit Banerjee is a friend of the detective,

Byomkesh Bakshi; that's why I am taking this precaution.'

Byomkesh let me go after fifteen minutes. I looked in the mirror and lo and behold, this was not Ajit Banerjee—this was a totally different person. With a fine moustache and French-cut beard, I looked ten years older and my complexion was darker. I became nervous.

'I hope the police wouldn't arrest me!'

Byomkesh laughed and said, 'Never! The police will never recognize you. If you don't believe me, go downstairs and ask someone you know if they can show you the house of Ajit Banerjee!'

I was even more frightened, 'No, no... There is no need for that! I am going out.'

As I was going out, Byomkesh said, 'You know what you have to do; you have to be careful only while returning, because you might very well be followed.'

'Is that possible?'

'Maybe... I will remain home. Come back as quickly as you can.'

After I came out on the stairs, I felt very uneasy for some time. When I found that no one was bothered by my disguise, I was relieved.

I became a bit bold too. There was a paan shop in the corner of the street from where I regularly bought paan. The Bihari shopkeeper always greeted me whenever I went to his shop. I went there and asked for paan. The man gave me the paan and took the money without even looking at me.

It was past five in the evening and was getting late. So I boarded a tram and got down at Esplanade. Soon I reached the spot. Although it was not a romantic mission, I felt quite excited.

But this excitement did not last long. It was extremely difficult to stand still at the appointed place where the traffic was like a flowing river. I was pushed several times by the crowd but I patiently stood there. There were other dangers of standing like a clown against a lamp post in a crowded street. There was a policeman at the crossing eyeing me suspiciously... Any moment, he would come and question me, 'Why are you standing there?' I quickly looked away and stared admiringly at the window of the big departmental store across the pavement. I hoped that I looked like a country bumpkin and not like a robber to be taken into custody.

I looked at my watch—five-fifty. If I could spend another ten minutes, I could escape. I waited impatiently… I concentrated on my pockets… I examined the pockets frequently and thoroughly, but there was nothing new there.

At last, it was six o' clock. I heaved a sigh of relief and walked away from the lamp post. Again, I examined my pockets—nothing there. I felt a great satisfaction to think that Byomkesh's conjecture was not correct. I felt that I had won a point over him. Thinking about all this, I walked towards the Esplanade tram depot.

'Babu, buy pictures!'

I hear this being whispered very near my ears. Startled, I looked around to find a lowly, decrepit-looking man wearing a lungi. He pushed an envelope into my hand, with obscene photographs in it. I knew that this was a popular but disgusting business in these areas. Angrily, I turned around to give back the envelope, but I could not find anyone around; the man in the lungi had vanished into thin air.

Bewildered, I was wondering what to do when I heard the sound of laughter. I turned around to see an elderly Anglo-Indian gentleman standing next to me. Without looking at me, he spoke in chaste Bengali in a very familiar voice, 'I see that you have got your letter. Now go home. Don't take the straight route. Go by tram from here to Bowbazar, from there by bus to Howrah crossing and then from there to our house.'

The tram for Circular Road came at that moment. The old gentleman boarded the tram and went off.

When I returned home after going around the whole city, I found Byomkesh sitting on an easy chair, smoking a cigar. I pulled out a chair and sat down.

'So Saheb, when did you return?'

'About twenty minutes back.'

'Why did you follow me?'

Byomkesh said, 'I had a reason to follow you. But I was not successful—I was a minute late. When you were standing near the lamp post, I was about five yards from you, near the departmental shop choosing a pair of socks. The person dealing with the "Thorn in the Flesh" must have suspected something, especially because of the way you were fidgeting and putting your hands in your pockets every two minutes. So he did not give the letter to you. After you left, I too came out of the shop, but I was about two or three minutes late. In the meantime, the man had done his work. When I reached you, you were standing like a fool with the envelope in your hand. How did you get the envelope?'

When I told him how I had got the envelope, he said, 'Do you remember the man? Did you look at him properly?'

I thought for some time and said, 'No, I don't remember anything, only that the man had a large mole by the side of his nose.'

Disappointed, Byomkesh shook his head, 'That is not a real mole but a false one—like your moustache and beard. Anyway, let's see the letter. In the meantime, you better go and wash off your makeup.'

When I returned after washing and having a bath, I was

amazed to see the expression on Byomkesh's face. He was walking up and down the room very quickly and his face was lit up with great joy. My heart too lifted seeing him so happy. I asked eagerly, 'Did you get anything in the letter... Did you read it?'

With great joy and enthusiasm, Byomkesh thumped my back and said, 'Only one little thing, Ajit, only a small thing. But I won't say anything to you now. My mind was like the Howrah Bridge—the roads had converged in the centre, but there was a little gap left; one small portion of the bridge was open in the centre. Today, that gap has been filled!'

'How has it been filled? What is there in the letter?'

'You read it yourself,' said Byomkesh, handing me the letter.

Besides the ugly pictures, there was a sheet of paper inside the envelope. I had seen it earlier but didn't have a chance to read it. Written on it in clear handwriting was the message, 'Who is the thorn in your flesh? What is his name and address? What do you want? Write clearly, do not hide anything. There is no need to sign your name. Put your letter in an envelope and on the tenth of March, at midnight, follow the road to the west of Kidderpore Race Course. A man will come from the front in a bicycle. He will be wearing motor goggles. So you will have no trouble recognizing him. As soon as you see him, stretch out your hand with the envelope. The bicycle rider will take the letter from you. After this, you will be informed about the next step. Come walking, and don't bring anyone with you. If you do, you will not meet the man.'

I read the letter thrice, carefully. It was indeed a strange and exciting letter. But I could not fathom why Byomkesh was so happy. I asked, 'What is the matter? I can't see anything!'

'You cannot see anything?'

'Whatever you assumed yesterday was correct. The secrecy and the desire of the man to function incognito seem a bit suspicious—that's all!'

'Oh my blind friend, can you really see nothing in the letter?' Byomkesh stopped suddenly—there were footsteps on the stairs.

'It's Ashu babu. Don't tell him anything about this,' he took the letter from me and put it in his pocket.

I was amazed to see the change in Ashu babu's appearance when he entered the room. It was unbelievable that a person could change so drastically within a day. His uncombed hair, his crushed clothes, lines on his face and dark rings under his eyes were proof that he was a totally broken man after the incident. Even yesterday, when he was so anxious after escaping from death by the skin of his teeth, he didn't look so devastated. He sank tiredly into an armchair and said, 'I had to give you some bad news—my lawyer Bilas Mallick is absconding.'

Byomkesh told him in a deep sympathetic voice, 'I knew that he was going to run away. Your friend in Jorasanko house has run away with him, I presume?'

Ashu babu was stunned for some time, 'You...you know everything!'

Byomkesh said, 'Everything. Yesterday, I went to your house in Jorasanko. I also saw Bilas Mallick. That woman was conspiring with him for quite some time, and you knew nothing about it. After you made your will, Bilas was curious to see your beneficiary. Curiosity soon turned into love, but they couldn't do anything till they got a good opportunity. Don't be sad, Ashu babu. It is your good luck that you have escaped from a disloyal friend and a fickle-minded woman. There is no fear for your life now. You can walk without fear on any street.'

Ashu babu agreed fearfully, 'What does that mean?'

Byomkesh said, 'It means exactly what you suspected but did not want to believe. They were trying to kill you—but not by themselves. In this city, there is a person whom no one knows or has ever seen, someone who has mercilessly killed five innocent people using a strange weapon. You, too, would have gone but luckily escaped, because you were destined to live long.'

Ashu babu sat for some time, covering his face with his hands. Then sighing deeply, he began his painful story, 'I am suffering for my own sins that I have committed at this old age. I can blame no one else. Till I was thirty-eight, I lived an innocent life. Then I went to Deoghar to see the famous Tapovan—the place where young ascetics take their vows of celibacy. Ironically, I saw an extremely beautiful girl there and fell madly in love. Athough, until now, I was averse to marriage, I was determined to marry her. But I got to know that she was the daughter of a prostitute and, therefore, marriage was impossible. But I could not leave her. I brought her to Calcutta, rented a house in Jorasanko and we began living together like husband and wife. I have regarded her as my wife for the past twelve years. I left all my property and money to her in my will. I thought that she too regarded me as her husband, but I was mistaken. I never suspected her. I did not realize that a prostitute's daughter could never be a loyal wife. Anyway, I have learnt my lesson in my old age.'

He was silent for some time and then said in a broken voice, 'Do you know where they have gone?'

Byomkesh said, 'No, besides it is better for you not to know where these two have gone; that road is not good for a person like you. You may be blamed by society, but I regard you with great respect. You are still simple and innocent at heart, although you have played with mud. That is why you should be praised. You are hurt now. But later, you will realize that this was the best thing that could have happened to you.'

Ashu babu said emotionally, 'Byomkesh babu, you are much younger than me, but the consolation that I have received from you is unexpected. No one shows any sympathy for a sinner—that is why the burden of the sin seems so heavy. But your kind words have lightened my heart. I am very grateful to you. There is nothing more to say; I will always be indebted to you.'

Our hearts were heavy after Ashu babu had left. Before going to bed, I asked, 'When did you know that the lawyer and the woman were trying to kill Ashu babu?'

Byomkesh looked at the ceiling and said, 'Yesterday afternoon.'

'Then why didn't you catch them before they ran away?'

'It was no use catching them. There was no proper evidence or proof against them that could be presented before a court of law.'

'But you could have gotten the name of the real murderer behind the gramophone pin mystery.'

Byomkesh smiled and said, 'If that was possible, I would not have tried to get rid of them.'

'You made them run away?'

'Yes, after Ashu babu luckily escaped from death. They were planning to run away as it is. I went to Bilas's house this morning and told him that I know a lot of things, and if he doesn't leave the city now, he will be caught by the police. The lawyer is an intelligent person—he took all of his client's money and left with his paramour by the evening train.'

'But what did you gain by making them run away?'

Byomkesh got up and yawned, 'Nothing much—only that I could mete out just punishment to a culprit. I had informed the Burdwan police, and by now, they must have caught Bilas Mallick with all his client's money. No one will be able to stop Bilas's two years of hard imprisonment, although he should have actually been hanged for trying to murder Ashu babu. Anyway, two years in prison is not bad.'

5

The next day, an unknown guest came to visit us. We had just finished our tea and were about to read the daily newspaper when there was a knock on the door.

Byomkesh raised his voice, 'Who is there? Come in!'

A good-looking and well-dressed young man entered the room. He was clean shaven, tall and slim, about thirty years of age, and had the looks of an athlete. He greeted us smilingly and said, 'Sorry to disturb you early in the morning. I am Prafulla Roy; I am an insurance agent.' Saying this, he sat uninvited on a chair.

Byomkesh said in a sour voice, 'We don't have money to make insurance policies.' Prafulla laughed.

There are some people who are good-looking, but as soon as they open their mouth, they look ugly. Prafulla was one of those people. He was probably addicted to paan—his teeth were stained with paan juice. I was surprised to see how such a good-looking face changed to an ugly one in no time.

Prafulla said laughingly, 'I am an agent all right, but I have not come to you in that capacity. Actually, even relatives lock their doors when they see us coming—and one can't really blame them! But you can rest assured that I have no such designs. Are you Byomkesh babu? I have come to get some private advice from you, if you don't mind.'

Byomkesh said in a displeased manner, 'If you want advice, you have to pay in advance.'

Prafulla took out a hundred rupee note at once from his wallet and said, 'What I am going to say is not private, but...' I was about to get up and go when Byomkesh said in a stern voice, 'Whatever you have to say, you can say in front of him.'

Prafulla said, 'Alright, alright, if he is your assistant, then there's no problem. What is your name... Ajit babu? I am indeed sorry. I did not realize that you are Byomkesh babu's friend. You are a very lucky man to be in the company of such a great detective and so fortunate to be able to help him solve strange and intricate mysteries. I am sure you don't have a single dull moment in your life. I sometimes feel it would be nice if I could join you too, leaving the boring job in the insurance company.' Saying this, he opened a box full of paan and took one.

Byomkesh was getting more and more impatient all this while. Now he said, 'If you could please tell us what advice you have come for, it will be convenient for me.'

Prafulla turned to him quickly and said, 'As you already know, I am an agent in an insurance company. I work for Bombay's Jewel Insurance Company; the company was pleased with my work and has given me charge of the office in Calcutta. I have been working here for the last eight months. The first two months went smoothly. Then a person turned up—I don't want to give any names—who was after me. I don't do business of small amounts; for such cases, I send my agents. But I personally go to the big clients. Now, this person began to spoil my business by poaching my important clients. Wherever I went, he would turn up there too—he even spread damaging rumours about my company. I found that I was losing all my important clients. About four or five months went by. My company began asking for explanations, but I just couldn't find a way to save the business from this man. I could have gone to court, but that would mean bad publicity and loss of money for my company. This man began sucking me like a leech. Another month went by... I could find no way out!'

At this stage, Prafulla opened his wallet and gave Byomkesh two carefully kept pieces of paper. Then he continued with his story: 'I don't think you noticed these advertisements that I came across about a fortnight back. It is only a five-line advertisement, but as soon as I read it, my heart jumped with hope and joy! A thorn in the flesh! Let me see if I can get rid of the thorn in my flesh! I was so desperate by then that I would not have minded seeking even supernatural help.'

I stuck out my neck and saw that it was the same advertisement about the thorn in the flesh.

Prafulla said, 'Did you read it? Isn't it interesting? Anyway, I went to the appointed spot on the appointed day, that is, the Saturday before the last. I stood resting against the lamp post like Lord Krishna resting against the Kadam tree. I can't express my uneasiness. There were pins and needles in my legs, but I saw no one. Disgusted, I turned to walk away when I found a letter in my pocket.'

He now gave the second piece of paper to Byomkesh and said, 'Read the letter, please.'

Byomkesh began reading the letter. I stood next to him. It was exactly the same letter which I got, only the date was different. Instead of Sunday, the time mentioned was on Monday, the eleventh of March, at midnight.

Prafulla gave us time to read the letter, then he continued, 'First of all, I couldn't understand how the letter had reached my pocket; then after reading the letter, my heart skipped a beat! I don't like mysteries…but the letter is full of them. I felt that there was a cruel plan hidden in the letter. Otherwise, what was the reason for this hide and seek? I don't know who the person is or what he looks like…but he has asked me to walk on a lonely road at midnight! Isn't the whole thing very suspicious? What do you think?' He looked at me for an answer.

But before I could talk, Byomkesh said brusquely, 'You don't need to know what he thinks. Just tell me about why you need advice.'

Prafulla was a little hurt, 'That is what I am asking. I don't know the sender of the letter, but he doesn't seem like a law-abiding person. So should I go to the appointed place? I haven't been able to decide anything for the last ten, twelve days. There is now only a day left. That is why I have come to you for advice.'

Byomkesh thought for some time and said, 'I cannot give you any advice today. Leave these two pieces of paper with me. There is still time; I will let you know tomorrow morning after thinking over the matter.'

Prafulla said, 'But I won't be able to come tomorrow morning, as I have to be somewhere else. Is it alright if I come tonight at eight or nine?'

Byomkesh shook his head, 'No, I will be busy tonight. I have somewhere to be as well...' Saying this, he looked askance at Prafulla and tried to change the topic, 'But you don't have to worry, if you come at four or four-thirty in the afternoon tomorrow, enough time will remain for your appointment at midnight.'

'Alright, I will come tomorrow,' saying that, Prafulla pulled out the box again and put two paans into his mouth. He offered the box to me and when I refused, he said, 'You don't take paan. It has become a bad habit for me—I can do without lunch and dinner, but not without paan. Alright, good day.'

He turned at the door and said, 'Should we inform the police about this? Maybe it would be better if the police found out everything about this man.'

Byomkesh suddenly lost his temper, 'If you go to the police, then don't expect any help from me. I have never worked with the police. You take your money back.' With that, he threw the hundred rupee note on the table.

'No, no! I only wanted to know your opinion; if you don't

like the idea, it's okay.' With these words, Prafulla beat a hasty retreat.

Byomkesh picked up the hundred rupee note after the man had left. He went into his library and closed the door. He does become very irritable at times. But if he is left alone then, he recovers from his bad mood quickly. I knew this about him. So, even though there were lots of questions I wished to ask him, I tried to concentrate on the newspaper.

After some time, I heard Byomkesh speaking on the phone; I heard a few English words. He spoke for nearly an hour. Then he opened the door and came out of the room. I observed that he was his old, amiable self again. I asked, 'Who did you call?'

He did not reply to my question but said, 'While you were coming back from Esplanade yesterday, someone had followed you.'

I asked, surprised, 'Really?'

Byomkesh said, 'Yes, definitely. But I give credit to his courage.' Saying this, he smiled to himself.

I didn't understand why following me was such a courageous act! Sometimes, it is difficult to understand Byomkesh; trying to understand him is like trying to solve a difficult puzzle. It was also useless asking him any questions, because he would refuse to answer until the time was ripe. So, without wasting words, I got up to take a shower.

The whole afternoon and evening, Byomkesh sat as if he had nothing to do. I asked a few questions about Prafulla; but he pretended not to hear me for some time, then suddenly opened his eyes and said, 'Prafulla Roy! Oh, the fellow who came this morning? No, I have not thought of any advice to give him as yet.'

He was smoking after dinner, as the clock struck ten. All of a sudden, he jumped up from his chair and said, 'Get up!

Get up, warrior! Get dressed for war. If we don't start dressing now, we will be late for our appointment.'

Surprised, I said, 'What appointment?'

Byomkesh said, 'Why? Have you forgotten your appointment with the "Thorn in the Flesh"?'

I stood up in fear and said, 'Sorry, I am not going there alone at night. You can go if you want to.'

'I will definitely go but so will you!'

'Is it a must? Why are you so concerned about the "Thorn in the Flesh"? It would have been much better if you worried about the gramophone pin mystery.'

'Maybe, but now I want to satisfy my curiosity. The gramophone pin mystery is not running away. Besides, Prafulla will come for advice… I need to have some matter and news to advise him about.'

'But in the letter, only one person has been asked to go, so the two of us can't go together!'

'I have worked that out. Now come to the other room; we are running out of time.'

Byomkesh dressed me up quickly in the library. I looked at the mirror. Last evening's gentleman had come back with his moustache and French-cut beard. Byomkesh concentrated on himself then. He did not put any makeup. He dressed in black, and wore a pair of black shoes. Then he positioned me at about five or six feet distance from the mirror. He stood behind me and asked, 'Can you see me in the mirror?'

'No.'

'Now walk forward, can you see me?'

'No.'

'Good! Our work is done. Only one thing is left.'

'What now?'

I had noticed that there were two china plates on the table.

A Thorn in the Flesh

They were ordinary plates—something like the ones in which snacks are served in restaurants. He took one, placed it on the left side of my chest and tied it tightly with a broad belt, saying the words, 'Be careful that it doesn't move; wear your coat on top and nothing will be seen.'

I asked with great surprise, 'What is all this?'

Byomkesh said, 'We have to wear our shield; don't be afraid, even I will wear it.' Byomkesh wore the second plate inside his waistcoat and buttoned it up to keep the plate in place.

We went out of the house in that strange gear at twenty past eleven. Just before going out, Byomkesh opened the cupboard and put a few things in his pocket. He also reminded me, 'Don't forget the letter; put it in a white envelope.'

We got a cab at Sealdah crossing. There were very few people on the streets, and most of the shops had closed. Our taxi moved fast.

We stopped the cab at the junction where the Kalighat and Kidderpore tramlines separate. The taxi left after we paid the fare. We looked around and did not find a soul on the road. The bright street lights made the silence even more eerie. It was ten minutes to twelve.

In the cab, we had already discussed what we would do, so we didn't have to speak. I walked ahead and Byomkesh followed me like a shadow in his black suit. His steps exactly shadowed mine about six inches behind me, but it seemed as if I was alone on the street. Although there were street lights, visibility was poor. There were no buildings on the two sides to reflect the light. So, it was impossible for anyone coming from the front to realize that there was someone behind me.

On one side were the tramlines; the trams had their last rides of the day a long time ago. On the other side were the white-painted railings of the race course. I was walking in the middle of the road. Far away, a clock struck midnight—other clocks all around began to chime as well. When the sound stopped, I heard Byomkesh whispering, 'Take the letter in your hand now.' I had nearly forgotten that he was behind me; startled, I took the letter in my hand.

I walked for about six or seven minutes. I was halfway to Kidderpore Bridge when at a distance in front of me, I saw a dim spot of light. I heard near my ear, 'He is coming, be ready.'

The light became brighter as it drew nearer. Behind it, within a minute, came a darker object, moving at great speed, on the pitch-black road. Soon, I could make out the bicycle rider. I stood with the envelope in my outstretched hand. The bicycle slowed down. I waited with bated breath. The bicycle was about twenty-five yards away from me now. I could see the rider wearing a black suit and motor goggles, piercing me with unblinking eyes.

The cycle now was coming towards me at a medium pace. When there was only about ten metres of distance between us, the bell of the bicycle rang a few times, and I felt a terrible blow on my chest and fell on the road. It was then that I realized that the plate tied to my chest had broken into pieces.

Something incredible happened within a second. As soon as I fell, Byomkesh came forward at lightning speed and jumped on the rider. The rider was totally unprepared for this, as he had not imagined that there could be someone behind me. Even then, he tried to escape. Byomkesh pushed him with his bicycle, and he fell on the ground. Byomkesh jumped on him and sat on his chest, clasping his wrists with strong hands. I got up to help Byomkesh, and found the infamous bicycle lying on one side of the road.

Byomkesh said to me, 'Ajit, you will find a strong silk cord in my pocket; tie his wrists securely with it.' I did as I was told.

Byomkesh then said, 'All right now! Ajit, don't you recognize this gentleman? He is our friend who visited us this morning—Prafulla Roy. If you want a more detailed introduction—he is the killer behind the gramophone pin mystery.'

Byomkesh took off Prafulla's goggles as he spoke.

I was left totally dumbfounded by the sudden turn of events. But even at this time, Prafulla gave his terrible stained-teeth smile and said, 'Byomkesh babu, please get down from my chest; I won't run away.'

Byomkesh said, 'Ajit, search his pockets. He might be carrying some weapon.'

I took out an opera glass from one pocket and a box of paan from the other. I opened the box and found that there were four paans left.

Byomkesh now climbed down from Prafulla's chest. The latter sat up, stared at Byomkesh and slowly said 'You are cleverer than me. I ignored your intelligence—but you didn't. It is stupid to underestimate the strength of your enemies. I have learnt this lesson too late in the day.' He smiled wryly.

Byomkesh took out a whistle from his breast pocket and blew on it; then he said to me, 'Ajit, pick up the bicycle and keep it aside; but be careful to not touch the bell—it is very dangerous.'

Prafulla smiled, 'You know everything. You are an unusual person. I was afraid of you—that is why I tried to trap you today. I thought you would come alone. But you have disappointed me! I was proud of my acting abilities, but you are a far better artist. This morning, you saw through my disguise and acting, but I only saw what was apparent. Anyway, my throat is dry; can you give me some water?'

Byomkesh said, 'Where will you get water here? You will have to go to the police station first.'

Prafulla kept quiet for some time. Then he looked hungrily at the box of paan and said, 'Can I have a paan? Of course, there is no rule of giving paan to a criminal but my throat is dry and a paan would help.'

Byomkesh made a sign and I followed him by putting two paans in Prafulla's mouth.

'Thank you,' said Prafulla. 'You can have the other two.'

Byomkesh was anxiously waiting for the police to arrive. The sounds of cars and motorbikes were drawing near every second.

Prafulla asked, 'You won't let me go?'

Byomkesh countered, 'How is that possible?'

Prafulla smiled vaguely and said, 'Will you hand me over to the police?'

'Of course!'

'Byomkesh babu, even an intelligent person makes a mistake. You won't be able to hand me over to the police...' Saying this, the artful dodger fell onto one side.

The uniformed police said, 'What's happening? Is he dead?'

Prafulla opened his eyes slightly and said, 'A bigshot has come for me... Too late, Sir, you haven't been able to catch me. Byomkesh babu, you should have taken the paan—we could have gone together then. I feel sad leaving a person like you behind.' Prafulla tried to smile but his effort turned into a grimace as he stiffened and his eyes closed.

A big truckload of police arrived. The commissioner came forward with the handcuffs. Byomkesh said, 'The bird has flown home; there's no need for handcuffs.'

ॐ

Byomkesh and I were sitting facing each other as usual in our sitting room. The light and breeze of a bright day were streaming in through the open window. Byomkesh was looking at a bicycle bell. On the table was a letter from the government.

Byomkesh opened the bell and looked admiringly at the intricate workings inside. 'What a genius he was! It is practically impossible to craft an amazing thing like this. Look at this spring which is wound tightly—it works as the gunpowder for this gun. How strong this spring is! So easy, yet so terrible! This small hole is the muzzle of the gun through which the pin comes out. If you press this, two jobs are accomplished—the bell rings and the pin shoots out. The sound of the bell covers the sound of the spring. You must remember that we discussed the other day that sound covers up sound, but what covers the smell of the gunpowder? There was no gunpowder in this gun. I realized how intelligent this man was that very day.'

I asked, 'How did you get to know that the "Thorn in the Flesh" and the gramophone pin were related?'

Byomkesh said, 'I didn't realize in the beginning. Later, unknowingly, both began to merge together in my subconscious. What is the "Thorn in the Flesh" telling us clearly? That he would get rid of any obstacle on the path to our happiness, of course for a few rupees. Although it is not written specifically, it is obvious that he won't do it out of the goodness of his heart. Now, just try to remember that all those who died from gramophone pins were all obstacles in the path of happiness for someone or the other. I don't want to cast aspersions on the relatives of the deceased—in any case, their guilt cannot be proved. But you must agree that the dead were wealthy, had no sons, and their heirs were either their nephews or their sons-in-law—relatives.

'So we can see that although apparently the gramophone pin and the "Thorn in the Flesh" are separate, they can easily be connected like two broken pieces of china. Another thing that attracted my attention from the very beginning is the similarity in the name of one thing and the working of the other. The advertisement is about a thorn, and people are being murdered with something similar to a thorn; isn't the similarity quite obvious?'

I said, 'Not to me... Maybe to you.'

Byomkesh shook his head impatiently and said, 'This is a very simple case of conjecture. As soon as I started investigating Ashu babu's case, all this became clear to me. The only problem was—who was the man? Here, we get the proof of Prafulla Roy's evil genius. Those who had paid Prafulla to kill didn't know who he was or how he accomplished his mission. His greatest protection was in keeping his identity hidden. I might have failed to catch him if he himself didn't turn up to test me out.

'I will have to explain a bit more. The day you went to keep the appointment with the "Thorn in the Flesh", he was suspicious of the way you were behaving; still he gave you the letter and followed you to the house. Now, he was sure that I had sent you there. He knew that I was investigating the case of Ashu babu. So he was certain that I knew quite a lot of things about him. Anyone else might have chickened out and fled the city, but Prafulla was very bold; he wanted to know how much I really knew and what I wished to do about the "Thorn in the Flesh". He was not in any danger of being caught because it was impossible for me to know and prove that he was connected to the gramophone pin as well as the "Thorn in the Flesh". But he made a slight mistake.'

'What mistake?'

'He did not realize that that morning, I was waiting for him to come, and I was certain that he would come to investigate.'

'If you knew, why didn't you get him arrested?'

'Don't speak like a fool. How could I arrest him without proving that he was the murderer? The only way was to catch him red-handed in the act; and that is what happened. Why else did we go with plates tied to our chests?

'Anyway, Prafulla realized after speaking to me that I knew a lot; but he didn't understand that I had recognized him. He decided that it was not safe for him if I remained alive. So he somehow saw to it that I went to the race course at that time of the night. He was sure that this time, I won't send you but go myself. He guessed that I was desperate to get to the bottom of the mystery. He was a little apprehensive about one thing: What if I take the help of the police? So just before going, he very cunningly mentioned the police. But I pretended to lose my temper as soon as I heard about the police. So, he went away happily, thinking that he had ensured my doom.

'Poor fellow! That was his gravest mistake. In fact, before dying, he even admitted his folly of disregarding my intelligence.'

Byomkesh was silent for some time before continuing with his story. 'If you remember, the first day that Ashu babu had come to our house, I asked him if he had heard any sound when he felt the blow on his chest. He said that he had heard only the sound of a bicycle bell. I did not give this much importance at that time. That is why there was a gap in my investigation. As soon as I read the letter given by the "Thorn in the Flesh" man, everything became clear in a second. I told you that I had found a keyword in that letter—the word was "bicycle".

'If one thinks deeply about it, one realizes that only a bicycle can kill so simply and unostentatiously. You are walking along the road and a bicycle rider comes along from the front, rings a bell for you to move to the side, then passes by, and you fall dead on the street. No one will suspect a bicycle rider, because he is clutching the handles with both hands. So how will he shoot? No one even looks at him when he passes by.

'If I remember correctly, the police tried very hard to catch the murderer promptly after Kedar Nandi was killed by the gramophone pin. As soon as he fell, the police stopped the traffic from all sides and searched every single person—but found nothing. I think Prafulla was very much there at that time, laughing to himself. The police, even in their wildest dream, didn't suspect a bicycle bell doing the work of a gun or a revolver.'

Saying this, Byomkesh looked somewhat affectionately at the bicycle bell. The brown envelope from the government fell at my feet from the table. I picked it up and asked, 'What has the police commissioner written to you?'

Byomkesh said, 'He has written a long letter, firstly thanking me on behalf of the government, then expressing sorrow at the suicide of Prafulla Roy; though this should have pleased him as it has saved a lot of expenditure on the part of the government to keep Roy in jail and to fight a court case against him. Then he promised to send the prize money for catching the culprit as soon as possible. No one has been able to identify the dead body of Prafulla because Jewel Insurance Company has said that they have one Prafulla Roy, who is now in Jessore on transfer. So, it is obvious that the name Prafulla Roy was a pseudonym, but he will always be Prafulla Roy to me. At the end of the letter, the Commissioner has asked me to return the bell because it is now the property of the government!'

I smiled, 'You seem very sorry to let it go!'

'Yes. I can even forego the prize money for a thing like this. Anyway, I shall have another memory of Prafulla—that hundred rupee note; it is more valuable to me than thousands!'

I said, 'Tell me Byomkesh, did you suspect that the paans were poisoned?'

Byomkesh said after a moment of thought, 'There is a grey area between certainty and uncertainty; that is the area of conjecture. Do you think it would have been right had Prafulla died on the gallows like an ordinary criminal? It is good that he died this way. He was a great artist, and showed it even when he was all tied up.'

I was stunned to observe the respect a detective had for a criminal.

At that very moment, a postman delivered a registered letter. Byomkesh tore it open and pulled out a cheque of a thousand rupees, signed by Ashutosh Mitra.

4

The Dart of Death
Agnibaan

Byomkesh threw the newspaper despairingly on my lap and said, 'No, there is nothing in the papers, nothing at all. I wonder why the newspaper owners don't publish blank papers; it would save them the expense of printing rubbish!'

I said sarcastically, 'Is there nothing in the advertisements either? You once said that advertisements are the most important part of a paper! It is in them that one gets the best news!'

Byomkesh lighted a cigarette sadly and said, 'No, there is nothing even in the advertisements these days. Only one fellow has put up an advertisement saying that he wishes to marry a widow. That sounds fishy to me; why specifically a widow and not an unmarried girl? There must be some ulterior motive behind that advertisement.'

'Maybe... Anything else?'

'An insurance company has given a large advertisement saying that they make joint policies for couples, and in case any one of the partners dies, the other gets all the money. These insurance companies have taken the charm out of even dying peacefully!'

'Do you think these companies have some bad intentions?'

'Maybe not the companies themselves, but they are putting ideas into people's heads. That is not a good thing either.'

'What do you mean by that?'

Byomkesh did not answer my question but sighed deeply, put up his feet on the table and kept on smoking.

It was winter, the time for Christmas vacation. The inhabitants of Calcutta had left the city for vacation and people from outside were visiting with great enthusiasm.

As usual, the two of us were drinking tea and dissecting the newspaper in the morning. Byomkesh was losing his patience after having nothing to do for the last three months. The days were being spent uselessly, reading uninteresting and useless news items. I could easily understand Byomkesh's condition, as I myself was facing the same state of boredom. But instead of consoling him, I tried to derive some enjoyment by mocking and scorning him.

This morning, I felt slightly sorry for him when I found him a victim of this desperate boredom. I realized that just as the body needed a diet to remain healthy, so will the mind. Moreover, it was not easy to be made fun of by a close friend. I felt repentant and began looking through the newspaper. I came across details only about lectures, seminars, etc. and a few advertisements of circuses and films! There was indeed a paucity of matters worth the attention of the discerning.

Five big meetings took place in Calcutta itself, while a huge science seminar was being held in Delhi. The long speeches made by the scientists there, as reported in a newspaper, were a cure for insomnia. I wondered why the scientists of our country talked so much instead of inventing something worthwhile.

As I was reading the review about the Science Congress in Delhi, my eyes lighted on a familiar name. He was a well-known scientist and researcher in Calcutta—Debkumar Sarkar. It was not that other Bengali scientists didn't deliver lectures; I am sure they did. But this name was familiar to us because he lived in our area, a few houses down the road from ours. We were not directly acquainted with him, but we knew his young son, Habul, quite well. In fact, he was quite close to us.

Habul is a great fan of Byomkesh. He is about eighteen or nineteen and is currently in the second or third year of college. He is a quiet, good-natured boy. He listened with rapt attention to anything that Byomkesh had to say, and was full of gratitude when we asked him to have a cup of tea with us.

I was a little curious to know what Habul's father had to say at the Science Congress. He had spoken about the financial crunch that the scientists of India had to face, may it be in their personal life or to pursue their research work. To distract Byomkesh, I said, 'This is what our Habul's father had to say in the Science Congress…' Byomkesh showed no interest and kept staring at the ceiling. I started reading:

> *It is true that no nation can develop without the help of science. Many feel that Indian scientists are lethargic and unintelligent—that we have no talent for inventing or discovering anything, and that is why we are not self-reliant. But the fact that this notion is totally wrong can be proved by our glorious past. The foundations of all new scientific inventions had been laid by the great scholars of ancient India. Mathematics, Astronomy, Architecture and Medicine are the four pillars on which modern scientific knowledge rests. The source for all these four branches of science is in our country.*
>
> *But we must acknowledge the fact that, in recent times, our great powers of invention are becoming weak. What is the reason for it? Are we mentally weaker than our forefathers? No. The reason why our genius is not flowering lies elsewhere. In ancient times, the great learned scholars used to pursue their studies under the patronage of great kings and emperors.*

They were not worried about pecuniary problems.

But what is the condition of scientific research in our country today? Neither the government nor the rich sponsors are bothered about scientists and their work. We have to depend on meagre university funds to pursue our research works—no wonder we cannot succeed.

Even then, I can declare proudly that if we were allowed to work without worrying about daily necessities, we would prove ourselves to be no less than any other nation. But in spite of this poverty, we have made so many successful experiments in our laboratories that one would be astonished by them—if one ever gets to know about them. There are many inventors who are trying to improve upon their inventions instead of revealing it to the world. But they are alone.

My point is—we need monetary help, sympathy and scope to do full-fledged research so that we may be successful in our efforts. We need…

'Be quiet!'

I was getting quite interested in what I was reading, when I was interrupted by Byomkesh.

'What happened?'

'We want this, we need this—what has he invented that he wants so much from the country?'

I said, 'His dissatisfaction is only a screen to cover up his inefficiency.'

A mocking smile replaced the expression of irritation on Byomkesh's face. He said, 'Habul seems like an intelligent chap. Being his father, how can Debkumar move around giving these useless, long lectures? That's what is surprising.'

I said, 'It does not follow that an intelligent child will have an intelligent father, and vice versa. Have you seen Debkumar?'

'I don't think so. I have never felt any pressing desire to meet him. But I have heard that he got married for a second time, which proves that he is stupid.' Byomkesh closed his eyes.

It was half past eight in the morning. I was getting tired of sitting, so I got up to ask Putiram, our servant, to give us another round of tea. Suddenly, Byomkesh sat up straight on his chair. 'There are footsteps on the stairs…' He listened with great alacrity for some time, then relaxed disappointedly again in his chair. 'It's Habul. But what's wrong with him? Why is he climbing up the stairs so fast?'

Within a minute, Habul threw open the door. His eyes were wide with fear and his appearance untidy. He was not very good-looking at the best of times, but now his unshaven face and dishevelled attire made him quite a sight.

I said, 'What has happened, Habul?'

He did not even hear what I said; his eyes were fixed on Byomkesh. He stood in front of Byomkesh and broke down in a fit of sobs, 'Byomkesh da, Rekha is dead.'

∽

Byomkesh led Habul to a chair. It was difficult to calm him down. The poor fellow was a mere youngster; he was totally devastated by the incident.

We were not aware that Habul had a sister. We were not really interested in his family details. We only knew that after the death of Habul's mother, his father had remarried. This stepmother had no love for her stepchildren; we somehow learnt that too.

After about five minutes, Habul regained his self-control and related the whole incident to us. Debkumar had gone to Delhi to attend the Science Congress. The only people in the house were Habul, his younger sister and their stepmother. In the morning, as usual, Habul had gone off to his room in the second floor to study. After eight, there was a great commotion downstairs. He came down quickly after he heard screams from his stepmother. He saw that the lady was screaming unintelligibly in front of the kitchen. Habul entered the kitchen and found his sister kneeling down in front of the kitchen fire. Habul asked her what had happened, and getting no answer, touched her. At once he realized that Rekha was dead—her body was ice-cold and, her limbs were stiffening.

Habul began weeping again, 'What will I do Byomkesh da?' My father is not at home, so I came running to you for help. Rekha is dead—how did such a thing happen?'

Seeing the terrible plight of the young boy, my eyes too moistened. Byomkesh tried to comfort Habul and said, 'Habul, compose yourself and tell me, what happened to Rekha? Did she suffer from heart disease?'

'I don't know that.'

'What was her age?'

'Sixteen years, two years younger than me.'

'Did she suffer from any sickness recently? Beriberi or something like that?'

'No.'

Byomkesh thought for a while and said, 'Let's go to your house. I can't make out anything unless I see for myself. Send a telegram to your father—he should come back at once. But you can do that later. First, you have to get a doctor. Doesn't Dr Rudra stay near your house? Come, Ajit.'

We arrived at Debkumar's house within minutes. The house was longish in shape, as if the houses on the two sides had pressed it upwards. There was only one sitting room on the ground floor besides the kitchen and bathroom. As we approached the doorway, we were greeted by a shrill voice constantly talking and complaining. Though there was fear and anxiety in the voice, there was no sorrow. We realized that it must be the voice of the stepmother.

An old servant was standing, stunned, outside the house. Byomkesh told him, 'Go and call the doctor from that house.' He ran to obey the order, relieved to find something to do. We entered the house with Habul in tow.

We found the owner of the shrill voice standing near the steps going upstairs. As soon as she saw two unknown males in her house, she quickly covered her head with her saree and went upstairs. I had a glimpse of her expression—it was one of fear and irritation.

Habul said softly, 'My mother.'

Byomkesh said, 'I know, where is the kitchen?'

Habul pointed towards the kitchen. A small courtyard was surrounded by some small rooms—the largest of them was the kitchen. In front of the kitchen, water was flowing from a tap, making the whole area slippery.

We entered the kitchen after taking off our shoes. The room was dark and no light entered it. Habul switched on an electric light. Then we could see the inside of the room.

Opposite the door were two fireplaces for cooking with coal. Both were full of coal but not lighted. A young girl was kneeling down in front of these unlighted fireplaces. It looked as if she was praying to an unknown deity. Her body was bent forward and her chin was touching her chest. She didn't look as if she was dead. Byomkesh felt her pulse carefully.

His expression said it all—the girl was dead. Byomkesh now lifted the face of the girl by placing a finger under her chin. Rigor mortis had started setting in—the face could be lifted only slightly.

The girl was pretty, fair and sharp-featured, and her lips

were a bit swollen. She looked older than sixteen years. A head full of hair covered her back; she must have opened her plaits to get ready for a bath. She was wearing a striped saree. There were three gold bangles in each of her hands, a pair of earrings and a thin chain around her neck.

Byomkesh studied her closely and then stood a little away to get an overall view. Then he came close by and lifted the girl's hands—her palms were smeared with soot. She had placed the coal into the fireplace. As Byomkesh was separating her fingers, a small thing fell on the floor. It was the remainder of a burnt matchstick. Byomkesh looked at it attentively and then threw it away. The left fist was holding a match box. Byomkesh opened the box and found a few sticks in it. He said thoughtfully, 'I guessed as much. She died while lighting the fire.'

Then he looked around the room. He examined the wet footsteps on the floor and said, 'No, there was no one else in the room when she died. Then a woman came in, and then Habul.'

Footsteps were heard outside. Byomkesh said, 'Probably Dr Rudra has come. Habul, bring him in.'

Habul went out. I asked Byomkesh softly, 'Have you understood anything?'

Byomkesh frowned and shook his head, 'Nothing, except that the girl did not realize even a second earlier that she was going to die.'

Habul entered the room with Dr Rudra. He was an elderly man and a well-known physician but was notorious for his bad behaviour. He was ill-tempered and behaved badly, even with the most serious patients. No one would have tolerated any other doctor with the same kind of behaviour, but since he was an excellent physician, people were forced to bear with him. But besides being a good doctor, he had no other human qualities. His complexion was very dark, his face was long and his eyes were bloodshot—expressing insult to anyone that looked at him. He refused to give respect to any human being. When he entered the room, it seemed as if the personification of arrogance had dressed up in a suit and arrived!

Habul pointed to his sister. Dr Rudra asked in a rough voice, 'What happened? Is she dead?'

Byomkesh said, 'Why don't you examine her?'

Dr, Rudra glared at Byomkesh and said, 'Who are you?'

'I am a family friend.'

He ignored Byomkesh completely and asked Habul, 'Who is this? Debkumar babu's daughter?'

Habul nodded his head.

There was an expression of curiosity on Dr Rudra's face. He looked at the girl and said, 'Is this Rekha?'

Habul nodded his head again.

'What happened?'

'Nothing…suddenly…'

Dr Rudra knelt down beside the girl, examined her pulse, looked at her eyes and, after getting up, he said, 'She has been dead for nearly two hours. Rigor mortis has set in.' He gave the verdict in such a voice as if the news would please the hearers.

Byomkesh asked, 'How did she die?'

'That can be determined only after an autopsy. I am leaving. My fee is thirty-two rupees; send it to my house. The police should be informed—it is not a normal death.'

The doctor then left the house.

∽

While coming out of the kitchen, Byomkesh said, 'Yes, the police should be informed to avoid further trouble. I know the inspector-in-charge of this area, Biren babu. I will inform him.'

He wrote a few lines on a piece of paper and sent the servant to the police station. Then he said, 'Don't move the dead body… Let the police do whatever they should.' He shut the kitchen door and said, 'Habul, I would like to see your sister's room.'

Habul took us upstairs. He seemed stunned with grief and fear by the suddenness of the incident. He was moving about and obeying orders like a puppet on a string.

There were about three rooms on the first floor—the last one was Rekha's. The other two belonged to Debkumar and his wife. Although Rekha's room was small, it was neat and clean. On one side was a small bed. Near the window was a writing table, and next to it was a small shelf full of Bengali books. There was a mirror hanging from the wall and below it were some clips and combs and ribbons. The room was a proof of the decency and good taste of the owner.

Byomkesh looked at everything, wandered around the room and then stood by the window. The window was just above the lane. On the opposite side was Dr Rudra's huge mansion and chamber. The house and the terrace could be clearly seen from the window. Byomkesh looked out for some time, then came back and pulled at the drawer of the table.

It was not locked, and so it opened easily. There was nothing much there—two exercise books, a small letter pad, a bottle of perfume, a needle and thread, etc. Byomkesh picked up a bottle and found a few tablets in it. 'Aspirin. Did she take aspirin?'

Habul said, 'Yes, she used to suffer from headaches.'

Byomkesh kept aside the bottle of medicine and began walking with a worried expression, then stopped near the bed. The bed was slept in. The quilt was rolled by the side of the bed, and the pillow had the impression of a head on it. I felt depressed when I saw this.

Byomkesh lifted up the pillow mindfully. A light green piece of paper was under it. Byomkesh looked at the paper—it was a letter. After hesitating a bit, he began reading the letter. I started reading it with him:

Nantu da,

Your father has asked for a dowry of ten thousand. It is impossible for my father to give this huge amount. So, we will not be able to get married. But I cannot think of marrying anyone else—you know that already. This house, too, is unbearable to me. Could you give me a little poison? There are so many kinds of medicines in your pharmacy. If you don't give me the poison, I will surely get it from somewhere else. You know how firm I am when I decide to do something.

Yours,
Rekha.

Byomkesh handed the letter to Habul after reading it. Habul started crying again after reading the letter. He said in a voice choked with emotion, 'I knew this would happen. Rekha has committed suicide.'

'Who is Nantu?'

'Nantu da is Dr Rudra's son. There was a proposal for marriage between Rekha and him. Nantu da is a very good boy, but that greedy old doctor asked for ten thousand from my father. My father was very annoyed.'

Byomkesh wiped his face with his hands and said, 'But... anyway.' Then he made Habul sit on the bed and kept a comforting hand on his back.

Habul said sobbing, 'Rekha was the only one close to me. I have no one else in the house. I don't have a mother and my father has no time for us—he is so busy.'

Byomkesh's soothing hands calmed him down after a while. Then Byomkesh said, 'The police are going to come just now.

I want to ask your stepmother a few questions before that.'

The stepmother was in her room. Habul went to call her. She covered her head with her saree and stood by the door of her room. We saw her properly this time.

She was about twenty-seven or twenty-eight, slim, tall and fair. She also had nice features; but in spite of these attributes, it was difficult to call her even passable, let alone good-looking. Her eyes were sharp below puckered eyebrows, and her lips had a sarcastic fault-finding twist in them. After seeing her disgruntled expression, I was sure that she was not happy at all in her marriage. She had no child of her own. As she was not kind, she couldn't accept her stepchildren either. There was another thing that I noticed. She suffered from an excessive obsession for cleanliness.

Byomkesh asked, 'Did you meet Rekha this morning?'

In response, the lady spoke a lot more than was needed. I realized that besides her other faults, she was also prone to being garrulous. To Byomkesh's one short question, she revealed nearly everything about herself and her household. The maid was absent that day, so she had asked Rekha to scrub the kitchen floor and light the fire. Usually, she did all the household chores herself. She hated asking her stepchildren to do any household work. But it was not possible to do all the work for such a big house. So, she had to ask Rekha to go to the kitchen, while she went to take a bath before cleaning her room. She did not notice what was happening in the kitchen but came straight up to her room, where she chanted some prayers. When she came down again, she found what had happened. She usually avoided anything to do with her stepchildren, but fate had decreed that all their problems were piled on her always. After this incident, everyone would blame her, especially when her husband would return. He was sure to create a great commotion; she was afraid to even think about it. As it was, he could not tolerate her and would be happy if she died.

When the flow of words had slowed down slightly, Byomkesh got in a word edgeways, 'Did you scold Rekha this morning for anything?'

This time, she was furious, 'I never use strong words on anyone—I don't come from that sort of a family. Right from the day of my wedding, I have lived with my stepchildren. I dare anyone to accuse me of misbehaviour with them. This morning, I sent Rekha to light the fire. She came into my room and said that there were no matches in the kitchen and took the ones from my shelf. I was scrubbing the floor of my room then. I told her that she was old enough to realize that she should not enter my room wearing unwashed clothes; why didn't she ask the servant to buy matches from the shop outside? That's all I said. If I have made a mistake, I ask everyone's pardon.'

Byomkesh said coldly, 'There is no question of you making a mistake. But why did Rekha come to your room to take the matchbox? Do you keep all the matchboxes in your room?'

She said, 'Yes, I can't sleep in the dark. I keep an oil lamp burning constantly, so I have to keep the matchboxes in my room. The lamp and the matchbox are kept on the shelf. Everyone knows about it. Rekha, too, knew about it.'

I peeped into her room and saw a lamp on the shelf. I also noticed that the room was so clean that even the few pieces of furniture seemed stiff with fear of cluttering the room. Even the photograph of Goddess Kali on the wall seemed to be hanging her tongue in shame for fear of spoiling the cleanliness of the room.

Frowning, Byomkesh asked, 'So that's the last time you saw Rekha alive?'

She replied, 'Yes!' and would have continued her monologue

had the servant not announced the arrival of the police. We went downstairs.

Inspector Biren babu and Byomkesh knew each other intimately. Each knew the other's worth. Biren babu was a middle-aged, short, intelligent and efficient officer. Moreover, he did not have the usual tendencies of most policemen to underplay the efficiency of others, nor did he suffer from unnecessary arrogance and pride. Byomkesh respected this man and took his help in some complicated cases. He knew a lot about underground goons and petty pickpockets of the city.

He asked Byomkesh, 'What's the matter, Byomkesh babu? Is it something serious?'

Byomkesh said, 'You judge for yourself,' and took him inside.

⌒

The body was sent for post-mortem. A telegram was also sent to Debkumar babu. We returned home at about two in the afternoon, after making all the arrangements. The short winter day was almost at an end by the time we bathed and had our lunch.

Byomkesh seemed distracted and unusually quiet. I had a sense of guilt for desperately wanting something to happen earlier in the day. Who knew that such a shattering incident would take place to satisfy our hunger for a case? I was feeling extremely sorry for young Habul.

Soon, it was evening. Byomkesh was staring out the window, quietly, with unfocussed eyes. I asked, breaking the silence, 'Then it is nothing but suicide, isn't it?'

Byomkesh seemed to wake up from his trance with a start, 'Are you talking about Rekha? What do you think?'

Although I was not absolutely certain, I said, 'What else but suicide? We could determine that from the letter.'

'True. But how did she commit suicide?'

'By taking poison—she had written that in the letter as well.'

'Yes, but how could she have the poison even before she got it? In the letter, Rekha had asked for poison, and the letter had not reached the intended receiver—it was still under her pillow. So where did the poison come from?'

I said, 'It is in the letter that if she did not get the poison, she would try other means to die.'

'But do you think she would have tried other means even before sending the letter?'

I was clueless.

Byomkesh said after sometime, 'Besides, no one commits suicide while lighting a fire. Her death was sudden—like a bolt from the blue. It was the dart of death... She had no chance even to move. The matchstick burnt into ashes in her hand!'

'How was such a death possible?'

'That's what I can't make out. I know that the most dangerous poison is hydrocyanic acid, which is very strong and acts like lightning. But...' Byomkesh went into deep thought.

I said hesitantly, 'I know about medical science, but is it not possible to die of a sudden heart failure?'

Byomkesh said thoughtfully, 'That's the one remaining possibility. Rekha used to take aspirins for headache... Maybe the heart had become weak without her knowledge. But no, I am not able to accept the theory of a heart failure, although all the clues seem to point that way,'

Byomkesh smiled awkwardly, 'I can't match my intelligence with the dictates of my mind and heart. I keep on feeling that there is more to it. It is not a natural death. There is some problem somewhere. Anyway, no use worrying about it today; everything will be clear once we receive the post-mortem report.'

The room had become dark, and so Byomkesh got up to switch on the lights. We heard a soft knock on the door. We were surprised because we didn't hear any footsteps on the stairs.

Byomkesh raised his eyebrows in surprise and said, 'Who are you? Come inside.'

An unknown young man entered silently. He was a good-looking man with a good physique, although his expression was shadowed with tragedy. We did not hear his footsteps on the stairs as he was wearing rubber-soled shoes. He came forward a few steps and stood hesitantly.

'I am Manmathnath Rudra.'

Byomkesh looked him up and down, 'So you are Nantu babu? Come in.' He pointed to the chair.

After sitting down, the young man said softly, 'Do you know me?'

Byomkesh sat facing him and said, 'I got to know your name recently. Do you want to know about Rekha's death?'

The young man said in a trembling voice, 'How did she die, Byomkesh babu?'

'We don't know that yet.'

He looked at Byomkesh with unnaturally bright eyes and asked, 'Do you suspect that she committed suicide?'

'Not possible.'

'Then did anyone...'

'We can't say anything definitely, just yet.'

Nantu covered his face with both hands and sat quietly for some time. Then he lifted his face and said, 'You must have heard that Rekha and I were supposed to...'

'Yes, we have heard.'

Manmath had kept himself in check so far, but now he broke down. In a choked voice, he said, 'I loved her since childhood. When Rekha was only six years old, I used to go to their house to play—I have loved her since then. Then her father sent the marriage proposal. My father gave such an impossible condition.

Even then, I had decided that I would marry her against my father's wish. I had a terrible argument with my father. He threatened to throw me out of the house. Even then, I...'

Byomkesh asked, 'When did you quarrel with your father?'

'At noon, yesterday. I told him that I won't marry anyone except Rekha. Whoever knew then that Rekha...but why did this happen, Byomkesh babu? Who will gain by murdering Rekha?'

Byomkesh was scribbling on the table with a pencil without lifting his face, he said, 'Maybe it would benefit your father.'

Manmath stood up in trepidation, 'Father...my father! No... no... What are you saying... My father?'

He looked vacantly with terror-filled eyes and then left the room unsteadily. I turned to Byomkesh to find that he was still scribbling on the table with great concentration.

⌇

We spent the whole morning the next day waiting for the doctor's report, which did not arrive. Byomkesh rang up the police station, but even there, no one could tell us anything.

At about four-thirty, Debkumar babu came to our house. Although we were not acquainted with him, we knew him by face. We offered him a seat. He had left Delhi as soon as he received Habul's telegram and had reached Calcutta at noon that day.

He was over forty but looked older than his age. He was stout, bald-headed and wore a pair of thick-lens spectacles. He looked like a vague and unmindful person, an introvert. His long coat—buttoned at the throat—and his round glasses were a familiar sight for his students. We would sometimes see him too. But this day, he looked worn down and depressed. There were dark rings round his eyes, and his round face looked drawn.

He looked through his thick lens at me and asked, 'You... are you Byomkesh babu?'

I pointed to Byomkesh. He said, 'Oh!' and kept the walking stick on the table.

Byomkesh uttered a few words of sympathy; Debkumar babu did not seem to have heard him. He looked around the room vaguely and said in a soft voice, 'I started out from Delhi at ten in the morning yesterday and reached at about two-thirty today—nearly thirty hours on the train.'

We were silent. He looked totally tired, both physically and mentally. 'I have heard about you, Byomkesh babu,' he said. '...from Habul. Thank you very much for being there in our time of trouble.'

Byomkesh said, 'Please don't mention it. Any good neighbour would have done what we did.'

'Maybe—but you are an efficient person.' Then he asked suddenly, 'What happened to my girl? Did you understand anything? No one is able to say anything at home.'

Byomkesh related all that he knew and understood to the grief-stricken father. Debkumar took out a cigar from his pocket absentmindedly, and then put it away on the table. I observed him closely and found he was concentrating so keenly on what Byomkesh was saying that he was totally unaware of what his hands were doing in that moment of nervousness. At one time, he took off his spectacles and stared unblinkingly at me with large, vague eyes. Then he put on his glasses again and closed his eyes.

After Byomkesh had finished relating his story, Debkumar kept quiet for a long while. Then he said suddenly in an animated manner, 'That scrooge, miser Dr Rudra had entered my house! He is capable of doing anything for money. He is a demon!' He stood up excitedly, holding the stick in his hand. His quiet expression changed to a wild and violent one.

He regained his calm after a few minutes. He was a bit

embarrassed when he saw how surprised we were. He cleared his throat and said, 'I will leave now, Byomkesh babu, I would like to thank you again.' Saying this, he advanced towards the door.

Upon reaching the door, he frowned and thought for a moment, then came back, 'If I had money, I would have employed you to find out the truth of this case. But I am poor—I have no money.' Byomkesh tried to say something but he waved his stick and said, 'I will not take anyone's service without payment. The police are investigating—let us see what they find. Besides, what is the use of investigating—I will not get my daughter back.' Without any greeting, he moved out of our door.

We sat quite stunned after this strange man had left. Heaving a deep sigh, Byomkesh said at last, 'One wrong notion has been corrected. I was under the impression that Debkumar babu does not have much affection for his children—that is wrong. At least he loves his daughter very much.'

Debkumar had left his cigar behind on the table. Byomkesh looked at it and said, 'Strange, unmindful person!' Then he began pacing the room.

I said, 'He hates Dr Rudra.' Byomkesh did not answer me.

Later in the evening, Inspector Biren babu brought the doctor's report himself. He said, 'The report is very disappointing. Even after repeated tests, the cause of the death could not be determined.'

We read the report. The doctor had written that there was no wound anywhere on the body. No poison was found inside the body either. Her heart was normal and strong—so she did not die of heart failure either. From whatever little could be ascertained, death had occurred when the nervous system got suddenly paralysed, but how that happened remained a mystery. The doctor had never come across this kind of death before.

Byomkesh sat with a frown with the report in his hand.

Biren babu said, 'This case will be presented to the coroner's court, and the verdict would be "Death due to unknown circumstances." Then the police may or may not take up further investigation. What do you think, Byomkesh babu, is there any use of investigating further?'

Byomkesh said, 'I don't know if it will be fruitful, but we should not give up the investigation.'

Biren babu looked at him interestedly, 'Why are you saying that? Do you suspect someone?'

'No, I don't really suspect anyone, but I feel there is some deep mystery behind it.'

Biren babu nodded his head in agreement, 'Even I feel that, Byomkesh babu. What do you think of his wife?'

Byomkesh remained quiet for some time and then said, 'Look, I don't think it is any use moving in that direction. If we want to unveil the mystery, we must find out the real cause of the death. Until we are sure of that, it is no use suspecting this person or that. Of course, we must remember that when the girl died, her stepmother and her brother were the only ones present in the house. But that must not deviate us from the real cause of the crime.'

'But the doctor has not been able to say anything definite!'

'The doctor has only examined the dead body, but we have seen many other things besides the dead body. So, it is not right to say that we would not succeed where the doctor has come a cropper!'

Hesitantly, Biren babu said, 'Maybe. You have been with the family of Debkumar babu right from the beginning, so I expect that you would like to see the end of it. Okay, we will consult each other at every step.'

Byomkesh replied with a smile, 'No. Debkumar babu visited

us just a while ago. He has thrown me out of this business!'

Surprised, Biren babu said, 'What do you mean?'

'Yes, he does not want me to work for him without any charge, and he is incapable of paying my fees.'

'Really! But I have heard that he gets a very good salary, so how is he incapable of paying your fees?'

'I don't know.'

Biren babu looked suspicious, 'I have to seriously investigate Debkumar's financial status. But why is he rejecting your help? Is he trying to shield someone?'

I laughed out loud. The idea that Debkumar babu was trying to protect someone by rejecting Byomkesh's help seemed an extremely improbable story.

Biren babu was annoyed, 'Why are you laughing?'

I was taken aback and asked, 'Have you seen Debkumar babu?'

'No.'

'You would have realized then what made me laugh!'

Biren babu got up to leave. He told Byomkesh before going, 'I will get to the bottom of this case—let's see if I can solve it. But I won't let you go either. Debkumar babu may have shut the door on you, but I will come to you whenever I need you, please remember that.'

Byomkesh felt happy, 'That's very nice of you. I will help you as much as I can. I have a hunch that we should start working from Dr Rudra's angle. Who knows? The solution to this puzzle might be lying there!'

5

Five or six days went by without any incident. Byomkesh became listless again. Reading newspapers in the mornings and staring at the ceiling vaguely in the afternoons seemed to be his only occupation.

Even Biren babu did not visit us. So, we were in the dark about how much he had progressed in his investigation. The only visitor we had was Habul. However much he tried, Byomkesh could not bring him out of his depression. His eyes were lustreless. He would sit there for a while, get up and slowly leave.

One fine day, after Habul's departure, Biren babu arrived. His expression told us that he had not been able to make much headway. Afternoon tea arrived soon. Sipping the tea, Byomkesh asked, 'Any news?'

Shaking his head unhappily, Biren babu said, 'None, really. There's not even a hint of a clue anywhere. But I feel sure that there is some deep problem in this case.'

Byomkesh asked, 'Did you find anything new about the cause of death?'

'I personally met the doctor who had given the report. Although he doesn't want to say anything beyond the report, I believe that he has a theory of his own. He strongly suspects that the death occurred after inhaling some poisonous gas. He didn't specify anything clearly though.'

Byomkesh thought for a while and said, 'I suppose you told him that she died while lighting the kitchen fire?'

'Yes.'

Byomkesh thought for some time and then said, 'Anyway, did you find anything new about Dr Rudra?'

'Yes, I found out that he is extremely wicked, hard-hearted and greedy. There is a rumour that he killed off a few of his patients suffering from tetanus while testing out an injection on them, which he had invented. It is true that there was a proposal of marriage between his son and Rekha. It is also true that he asked for a hefty dowry, which Debkumar could not pay. So the talks did not proceed. The doctor's son is a nice boy. He had a violent argument with his father…but in the meantime, the girl died. The boy has left his father's house. He feels that his father is somehow connected with the death.'

The news that Manmath had left his father's house was new to us. We had already heard the rest of the news. Byomkesh asked, 'You had said that you would find out about Debkumar's financial status, have you done that?'

'Yes, his financial situation is not good. He doesn't have any debt, but it was impossible for him to spend such a large sum for his daughter's wedding. He is an impractical man. You will be surprised to hear that a major part of his monthly salary goes into paying the premium of an insurance policy. He has made a policy for a huge sum, and that too at this elderly age… So after paying the premium, very little is left of the salary at the end of the month.'

Byomkesh was surprised, 'Has he taken such a policy for a huge sum only for himself?'

'No, it is a joint policy for himself and his wife. He made the policy only a year back. It's his second marriage and his wife is much younger than him. He probably thought that he should leave her something in case he dies. This money won't go to any other inheritor.'

Byomkesh asked, 'Anything else?'

Biren babu replied, 'I have appointed people to shadow Habul. He has changed a lot. He hardly goes to college these days. He spends most of his time sitting alone in parks. He comes to you, too, as I found out.'

I noticed a sudden change in Byomkesh; his relaxed attitude had changed into one of acute alertness. It was after a long time that I saw that expression of excitement in his sharp eyes. I could understand nothing but, I started feeling excited as well.

Byomkesh did not expose anything. In the same dull voice, he said, 'You can leave out Habul. Are you going? Will you be at the police station? I will ring you up, if necessary.'

A little surprised, Biren babu left our house. After he went, Byomkesh paced around the room several times; I noticed the same old glint in his eyes. I was about to ask him why he had sort of made Biren babu leave the house so abruptly when he took a shawl from the chair and said, 'Let's go for a walk. My head is getting worked up in this closed room.'

We went out together.

Byomkesh started walking so frantically fast that it seemed to me that he wasn't completely conscious about his external surroundings. I was afraid that he would meet with an accident and I was desperately trying to save him from such a predicament. But he proceeded without decreasing his speed, banging into an old man, pushing over a young girl carrying books—like the unstoppable chariot of Lord Jagannath. In truth, I had never seen him so absentminded and unaware of his whereabouts. I understood that he was pursuing a definite purpose, but how would the poor pedestrians know what was going on his mind?

We arrived at College Square through frowns and abuses. The area was full of laughing and chatting students. I didn't hesitate any longer and pulled Byomkesh into the Square. Here at least, he won't trample old men and young girls! These young students would easily pardon his impoliteness.

Byomkesh was still thinking deeply, quite oblivious of what was happening around him. His shawl was falling off his shoulders, but he was unaware of it.

I began thinking… What had Biren babu said to make Byomkesh's mind react like a superfast train? Was he nearing a solution to the mystery of Rekha's death?

I did not realize then how close we were to the solution.

After walking in this manner for half an hour in the Square, Byomkesh slowly regained his calm and came back to reality. He asked me in a matter-of-fact voice, 'Today, Debkumar babu is leaving for Patna, isn't he?'

I nodded my head.

'He can't go...' Byomkesh looked ahead and began walking fast towards a bench surrounded by a crowd of students. They were talking excitedly; others were trying to peep into the crowd to see what had happened.

On reaching there, Byomkesh asked a boy, 'What's the matter here?'

The boy said, 'I can't make it out; I think someone died while sitting on the bench.'

Byomkesh pushed through the crowd. I, too, went with him. We saw a young boy sitting on the bench—he looked as if he had fallen off to sleep while sitting. An unlit cigarette was hanging from his lips. He was holding a matchbox in his hand.

A student felt his pulse and said, 'He is dead.'

It was getting dark. We could not see anything clearly in the crowd. Byomkesh pushed up the face of the dead boy with a finger under his chin. Then he let it go quickly, as if struck by lightning.

I could hear my heart hammering against my chest. The dead boy was Habul.

ഗ

The police came soon. We gave them the address of Debkumar babu and left. The street lights were on by then. We walked quickly towards our house. Byomkesh uttered several times in a terror-filled, hushed voice, 'What a revenge fate has taken! What a cruel jest!'

My reasoning power was numbed by the chain of terrible

events. But in spite of the deep sorrow that I felt, I thought if there was a life after death, Habul must have met his very dear sister, whose death he was mourning so deeply.

After reaching home, Byomkesh went into his room and shut the door. I could hear him talking on the phone.

He came out after an hour, slumped down tiredly on a chair and asked Putiram to give him a cup of tea. I did not want to bother him with questions. I knew that the grand finale of this tragic play would be enacted soon.

Biren babu came at about eight-thirty in the evening. Byomkesh asked, 'Have you brought the warrant?' Biren babu nodded his head in affirmation. We went out.

It took us three to four minutes to reach Debkumar babu's house. The house was silent and dark. There was light only in the sitting room below.

Biren babu knocked on the door, but no one answered. He pushed open the door that was not locked from the inside. We entered the room.

Debkumar was sitting like a statue on the divan. He looked at us with bloodshot eyes. Then he gave us a strange, bitter smile and said in a soft voice, 'The entire thing has misfired.'

Biren babu walked forward and said, 'Debkumar babu, there is a warrant in your name.'

Debkumar seemed to come out of a trance. He looked at the uniformed policeman and said, 'Good, you have come. I was going to the police station myself.' He stretched his hands out, 'Put on the handcuffs.'

Biren babu said, 'There is no need for that. I must tell you on what charges we are arresting you,' and started reading out from the official paper which he had in his hand.

Debkumar babu became unmindful again. He searched for something absently in his pocket and said, 'It must be fate, or else why should Habul use the same matchsticks too? Look at what I had planned and see what has happened. I had dreamt that I would arrange a good marriage for Rekha. I would make a huge, modern laboratory for myself and I would send Habul abroad for higher studies.' He took out a cigar from his pocket and put it between his lips.

Byomkesh quickly took out his own matchbox and lighted the cigar and then said, 'Debkumar babu, you have to hand over that matchbox to us.'

Debkumar again became aware of his surroundings. He looked at Byomkesh and said, 'You have come, Byomkesh babu? Don't be afraid, I won't commit suicide. I have killed my daughter and I have killed my son. I want to be hanged like a criminal.'

Byomkesh said again, 'Then give us the matchbox.' Debkumar pulled out a matchbox from his other pocket and threw it on the table, 'Take it, but be careful. It is dangerous. Each stick is a dart of death. Light one and you are finished.'

Byomkesh gave the matchbox to Biren babu, who carefully put it in his pocket.

Debkumar continued his monologue, 'What an invention I had made! Death would be instant, and there would be no clue. It would have made a path-breaking change in modern warfare. But everything has been in vain...' He heaved a sigh which seemed to break his heart.

Biren babu said softly, 'It is time to leave, Debkumar babu.'

'Let's go,' Debkumar got up immediately.

Byomkesh asked, feeling a bit awkward, 'Is your wife home?'

'Wife?' Debkumar's eyes were like a lunatic's. His loud laughter echoed in the small room. 'After I am hanged, she will get all the money from the insurance company! Isn't that a joke? Let's go.'

Byomkesh gently put Debkumar into the police van. Biren

babu and the two constables sat next to him.

Debkumar said from inside the van, 'Byomkesh babu, you tried to solve the mystery of my Rekha's death. Thank you so much!'

The van went off, leaving us standing on the street.

⁂

None of us could talk about the painful case for a few days. On the evening of the third day, Byomkesh began talking about it on his own.

'There is a saying, "Vengeance coming home to roost"; that's what happened to Debkumar babu. He wanted to kill his wife, but as fate would have it, for both times, his dart of death struck his very daughter and son.

'Debkumar had unexpectedly made this invention. But due to a dearth of funds, he could not develop or use this invention in the proper way. It was an invention which could not be patented, because it couldn't be used in ordinary day-to-day life. But if warmongering countries had any inkling about the formula, they would start producing this terrible weapon in their own countries. The original inventor would then be quite helpless and would not get anything for his invention.

'So, for the timebeing, Debkumar babu kept absolutely quiet about the invention. First of all, he needed money. A lot more research work was needed to find out the full and correct use of this invention. But from where would he get the money? To conduct such large-scale experiments in secret, he needed a big laboratory of his own, and that entailed a lot of money as well. He was desperate—where would he get the money?

'In the meantime, Debkumar babu's wife was making life miserable at home. Scientific experiments meant a great deal of mental pressure. He wanted some peace at home—but that was totally lacking. This harsh, heartless and quarrelsome woman was driving him mad. This is my assumption. Debkumar babu was not a cruel or hard-hearted person—he was driven to what he wanted to do. He would have been satisfied if he was just left in peace.

'It is not a normal feeling to want to kill one's wife. So, he had really reached the limit of his patience. When he invented this terrible thing, the first person he thought of probably was his wife. He started to play with fire mentally. Then the advertisement of the insurance company's joint policy project came as an answer to all his problems. It was a joint policy for both the husband and wife—in case of the death of one, the other would be the beneficiary.

'Where would he ever get such a chance? If he could make such a policy and kill his wife with his invention, then he would get the money to build his laboratory; and he would also get rid of his wife, without anyone ever guessing how she had died.

'Debkumar babu made a policy for a huge amount. Then he bided his time with great patience. The insurance company would become suspicious if he did anything in a hurry. A year went by when he decided to use the dart of death during this Christmas vacation.

'The poison that he had invented was like an explosive. It was quite harmless in its natural state, but as it came in contact with fire, the poison turned into a gas. If the tiniest particle of this gas was inhaled, it would mean sure death. The whole nervous system would be paralysed.'

'Debkumar babu found an excellent way of applying the poison on his wife. His scientific brain mixed this poison with gunpowder at the tip of the matchsticks. He prepared a few sticks in this way—how he managed to do this will be known only to him. Whoever would light these particular matchsticks would inhale the poison and die instantly. He began to get ready for the Science Congress in Delhi. Just before going, he left a solitary poisonous matchstick in the matchbox in his wife's room. He knew that his wife needed to light a lamp every night, as she could not sleep without a light in her room. This box of matchsticks was not usually taken from her room by anyone else. So, she would be the one to light that fatal matchstick some day or the other. At that time, he would be far away in Delhi, beyond all suspicion.

'Everything went off right, but fate smiled at his scheme. It was Rekha who died.

'He came back from Delhi. This time, he was very bitter and more determined to get rid of his wife. His warped mind blamed his wife for Rekha's death. A few days passed. He kept another deadly matchstick in his wife's matchbox and got ready to go to Patna.

'This time, of course, he could not go to Patna. Habul used to smoke. Maybe his own matchbox was empty... So he took a few matchsticks from his stepmother's matchbox and went out. You know the rest.

'The poison which Debkumar babu invented spread over his entire life.'

Byomkesh heaved a deep sigh of sorrow.

I asked after some time, 'When exactly did you know that Debkumar babu was the real culprit?'

Byomkesh replied, 'As soon as I heard that he had made an insurance policy for a huge sum. Before that, I could not understand why anyone should wish to murder Rekha. Who would benefit from her death? I couldn't get any satisfactory answer to that question. I did not realize then that Rekha was not the target of the murderer.

'But I got a small clue from another direction. When Rekha's body was examined, no poison was found. So the only conclusion I could come to was that whatever poison Rekha had died of was unknown to doctors and scientists. It could be a new invention! You must remember Debkumar babu's lecture in Delhi at the Science Congress, the one that you had read out to me. He had claimed there that many Indian scientists had discovered and invented many things in their small laboratories but couldn't do further experiments because of the lack of funds. I had taken his words for mere rhetoric then. Who would have guessed that he had really invented something so momentous? He was so excited about it that he couldn't stop himself from dropping a hint in his lecture.

'But the point was—how did this new invention come about? We know two scientists who were involved in this case—Dr Rudra and Debkumar. One of them was the inventor of this unknown poison. Dr Rudra was the primary suspect. He was a horrible man and was not happy about his son's involvement with Rekha. He had killed a few patients—as rumour went—while experimenting with one of his inventions. Moreover, he had greater chance of handling poison in his pharmacy. Besides, even if Debkumar babu was the inventor, why would he use the poison on his daughter? So, all my suspicions fell on Dr Rudra. But somehow, I was not fully satisfied. Dr Rudra was a wicked man, no doubt, but would he have killed off a girl for such a small reason? Besides, if he did wish to kill Rekha, how would he get to her? It was obvious on that day that he had not even seen her earlier.

'I was gradually coming around to the conclusion that a poisonous gas was responsible for Rekha's death. If you remember, Rekha had a burnt matchstick in one hand and a matchbox in another. So it was obvious that she died after lighting the matchstick. This incident may be totally coincidental, or there may be reason to be suspicious. Debkumar babu was very clever. He kept only one matchstick in the box, so that nothing would be found in case, after the incident, all the matchsticks were tested in the laboratory. Actually, I had brought that matchbox home and even got the contents tested—but found nothing. Even in the case of Habul, there was only one matchstick with the poison in that whole box. But just see what fate had in store for him! He put that very matchstick in his box and struck it to light his cigarette while sitting on the bench in College Square.

'Ajit, you're a writer. Don't you see an allegory in the story? The day man invented a weapon to kill his enemy is the very day he had struck his own death knell. In modern times, every other country is trying to find nuclear weapons to destroy the other. One day, it will recoil on the originator—like a boomerang!

'The human race is creating Frankensteins who will eventually destroy their creators.'

I could not see Byomkesh in the growing darkness of the falling dusk. In the faint light of the room, his words sounded menacingly prophetic.

༄

A few months later, the court case against Debkumar babu came to an end. He vehemently refused to disclose the formula of the poison which he had invented.

Biren babu, the inspector-in-charge of the case, gave us a frantic call two days after the case had closed. 'Terrible news, Byomkesh babu! Debkumar's lethal matchbox was displayed as an exhibit in the court case. It was handed over to the court authorities by the police. That box is missing!'

5

The Vanishing Trick
Manimandan

A valuable stone-set necklace had been stolen from the house of the famous jeweller, Rashamoy Sarkar. I saw the news in the latest-news column in today's paper.

At about eight in the morning, the telephone bell rang.

An unknown, anxious voice said, 'Hello...Byomkesh babu?'

I said, 'No, I am Ajit, who is speaking?'

'I am Rashamoy Sarkar. Could I speak to Byomkesh babu?'

I knew at once that Byomkesh would be requested to catch the thief.

I said, 'He has gone for his bath. I read in today's paper that a necklace has been stolen from your shop.'

'Not from the shop but from my house. Are you Ajit Banerjee, Byomkesh babu's friend?'

I said, 'Yes... You may tell me whatever you want to tell Byomkesh.'

He was quiet for some time, then he spoke again, 'The price of the necklace that has been stolen is a few lakhs. I suspect a servant, but there is no proof. I have called the police, but I need Byomkesh babu too. I know that he is the only person who can find the necklace for me.'

I said, 'Why don't you come over? In the meantime, Byomkesh will become free as well.'

Rashamoy said, 'Please, why don't you two come over to my house? I suffer from acute arthritis and can hardly move.'

I was a little hesitant. I have never seen Byomkesh going to a client's house first. Those in trouble are the ones who rush to him.

I told him, 'I will ask Byomkesh.'

Rashamoy began pleading, 'Please ask him not to refuse. Make sure you come—that is my ardent request. I am sending the car; you won't have any problem.'

'Alright.'

'Thank you! Thank you. I'm sending the car just now.'

After a few minutes, a huge Cadillac stopped in front of our house. I told Byomkesh everything as soon as he came out of the bathroom.

⌒

Rashamoy babu had about five or six jewellery shops all over Calcutta, but his own ancestral house was in Bowbazar. Soon, the car stopped in front of the house.

His house was an old-fashioned one. It went up to three storeys right from the edge of the footpath. There was a door that opened to a staircase in the middle of the building. There were two lines of shops by the two sides of the door. The house owner occupied two floors on top. The door was locked. As soon as the car stopped, the door opened and a young man came to take us in. He was well-dressed, good-looking and about twenty-seven or twenty-eight years of age. He greeted us and said, 'I am Monimoy Sarkar. My father is waiting for you upstairs. Please follow me.'

We went upstairs. There was a kitchen, servants' quarters, store room and a drawing room on the first floor. We kept climbing to the third floor. The master of the house lived there with his family.

We realized how wealthy the family was when we reached the second floor. There was a foreign lock on the door and a brocade curtain hung on the door. The floor was covered with a beautiful and thick Kashmiri carpet, and the drawing room was decorated with expensive Kashmiri furniture, wall decorations and tapestry work. But the room was a bit untidy. Monimoy took us into the room and said, 'Father, Byomkesh babu has come.'

We saw that Rashamoy babu was sitting on a chair and had stretched out his legs. A young married woman was sitting at his feet and massaging his legs.

Rashamoy babu was about fifty, a little heavyset and his face had an expression of determination. He tried to get up from the chair when he saw us but quickly sat down again. He first looked at me and then at Byomkesh, and greeted him first, 'Oh! Come in, Byomkesh babu. I am feeling harassed due to a lot of things. Anyway, now that you have come, I am feeling relieved. Please sit down, Ajit babu.'

I realized that he was an intelligent and perceptive man because he realized who Byomkesh was between the two of us, without having met us before. We sat next to each other on the sofa. Byomkesh said, 'You are suffering from arthritis. It is not a fatal ailment, but very painful.'

Rashamoy replied, 'I am otherwise a healthy person, but this arthritis has debilitated me. I used to play football in my younger days but I broke my right toe. Now, after so many years, that broken toe is giving me trouble, especially if it is a cloudy day. Never mind me.' He addressed the young lady, 'Go and bring some tea for these gentlemen.'

He then turned to us and said, 'She is my daughter-in-law.'

The girl was beautiful but looked anxious. She started getting up when Byomkesh stopped her, 'No, no, we have just had tea at home—you look after your father-in-law.'

Rashamoy smiled affectionately at her. She sat down again. He said, 'Monimoy, bring cigarettes for the gentlemen.'

When he left the room, the old man looked at his daughter-in-law and said, 'She is a very good girl. My wife has gone on a tour of holy places with my younger son, so she is looking after the entire household. But of course, I am not in the habit of making her massage my feet...but the servant...'

His tone of voice changed, 'Let's not waste time. I'll get to the point immediately. You have taken all the trouble to come to my house; I shouldn't waste your precious time. Byomkesh babu, a terrible thing happened in my house last night—something which had never happened earlier—a diamond necklace...'

Byomkesh said, 'Please, start from the beginning. Please don't shorten your account, give every detail.'

Monimoy opened a 555-marked tin of cigarettes and offered it to us. He moved to the window and stood there. Rashamoy began his story, 'I have five jewellery shops in Calcutta. It is a big business—with a yearly transaction of lakhs of rupees. I have many old, faithful and trustworthy workers. When I am alright, I look after the business; but for the last two years, Monimoy has also started looking after it.

'We do business even outside Calcutta; in fact, we have a network throughout India. We have business transactions with all the big jewellers of Bombay, Delhi and Madras. Sometimes, we buy precious stones from them, and sometimes they buy from us. Besides that, we have a lot of customers too; this ranges from royalty to middle-class people.

'About a month back, a renowned jeweller from Delhi called Ramdas Choksi approached me. He had received an order from a royal house in Rajasthan for their daughter's wedding. The order went up to lakhs of rupees—but he couldn't make all the ornaments himself due to the lack of time. So he wanted me to make a diamond necklace worth lakhs of rupees. I had to complete it within a month and send it to Ramdas's house.

'The necklace was ready. I wanted to hand it over to him myself. But since last Tuesday, I have been down with pain. I could not send such an expensive item through my workers. So, I decided that Monimoy should take it with him. He was supposed to leave for Delhi today.

'For the last few days, I couldn't go out of the house. Monimoy was looking after the business. The necklace was in the vault of one of the bigger shops. It was only yesterday afternoon that Monimoy brought it home.

'Now let me tell you something about my house. My wife has gone on pilgrimage with my younger son, Hiranmoy; now they are in South India. Monimoy, his wife and I are living in the house now. Two servants, the cook and the driver, and my own attendee—Bhola—live on the first floor. At present, these are the people living in the house.

Last evening, Monimoy brought the necklace home. I was sitting on this very chair while Bhola was massaging my feet. Moni gave the case to me and said, 'Take this, Father.'

I told Bhola to leave. I opened the case and examined the necklace—everything was alright. Then I called my daughter-in-law and asked her to pack the box nicely with cloth. She brought a piece of material and stitched the box inside it, here in this room.'

Byomkesh interrupted, 'What was the size of the box?'

Rashamoy looked here and there. Monimoy pulled out a book from the bookshelf and gave it to Byomkesh, 'This was the size of the box.'

Rashamoy said, 'Yes, that was the size. But of course, the box was made of crocodile skin and the inside was lined with expensive velvet.'

Byomkesh looked at the book attentively and gave it back to Monimoy.

Rashamoy continued his story, 'Then Moni went off to the club after having a cup of tea. I took the box to the office room. The room next to this one is my office. When I have to work at home, I do it there. There is a secretariat table, and in the drawers of the table, I keep important documents. I kept the box in one of the drawers. There is an iron vault in the house, but my wife has taken the keys to it by mistake.

'It was my fault… I shouldn't have kept such an expensive item in an open drawer. But the arrangement in my house is such that there was really nothing to fear. The servants stay on the first floor and never come here unless called upon; no one comes to this floor on their own. So I never thought that the box would be stolen from here.

'I had my dinner at about nine at night. Our dining room is on the first floor, but because I am suffering from pain at present, my daughter-in-law brings my food up here these days. I had my dinner and started reading a book. My daughter-in-law also had her dinner. Moni often comes back late from the club, so she kept his food covered in the bedroom.

'At ten, I rang the bell to call Bhola and then went to bed. He massages my body before I go to sleep and when I go off to sleep, he too leaves.

'Bhola is very efficient. He has been working with me for the last one and half years. He does all my work and looks after all my needs. Last night, too, he massaged my legs, and after I fell off to sleep, he, too, left, I don't know when.

'Suddenly, I woke up to Moni calling for me. He was bending over my bed and calling, "Father, Father!" I got up with a start. When I asked what happened, Moni said, "Where did you keep the necklace?" I told him it was in the drawer of the table. He said, "But it is not there!"

'I quickly went to the office room and pulled out the drawer—the box, indeed, was not there! I looked into all the drawers; it was nowhere. You can easily understand my mental state. I asked my son how he got to know that it was not there. He said...'

Byomkesh stopped him and asked Monimoy, 'What was the time then?'

Monimoy replied uneasily, 'Nearly midnight—five or ten minutes to twelve.'

Byomkesh said, 'You suspected at midnight that the necklace was stolen—why? Please tell me everything.'

Monimoy became very uneasy; he gave his father a surreptitious look and started speaking hesitantly, 'I came back quite late last night. A bridge competition was going on in the club. I...'

Byomkesh asked, 'Where is the club... What is it called?'

'It is called "Sports Club". It is only a five minutes' walk from home. There is all kinds of arrangement for sports there—cards, chess, table tennis, billiards, etc. Yesterday, the bridge competition came to an end, so...'

'Do you walk to the club?'

'Yes, it is close by. I came out of the club at quarter to twelve. The streets were empty. Just opposite our front door, there is a lamp post. When I was about thirty or forty yards away from our house, I noticed that all the shops had closed, but a man was standing right in front of our door. On other nights, I return home by ten, but the front door is locked before that. But it was open yesterday and I became a bit suspicious. I came in and closed the door from the inside. The servants were sleeping.

'As soon as I reached the second floor, my wife opened

the door for me. You must have noticed that the lock on the second floor door is such that it is locked from the inside—it can be opened from the outside only with a key. I told my wife that I saw a man outside our house; she said she too had seen someone.'

Byomkesh looked at the young wife, 'Even she saw the man?'

The girl blushed shyly, Rashamoy encouraged her to speak, 'Don't be shy, my dear, tell him all that you saw.'

The young girl began speaking haltingly, 'Last night, he was late coming back home, so I stood by the window looking out at the street. Suddenly, I noticed a man standing on the footpath. I tried to bend down and look but I couldn't see clearly. Then the man seemed to vanish. I felt the man had entered through the door. Just at that moment, I saw my husband coming towards the house… It seemed to me that the man had seen him and entered the house. Then I went and opened the door on the second floor and my husband came in.'

'Did you recognize the man?'

'No, I couldn't see his face from upstairs but I felt like it could be one of the servants.'

'Then what happened?'

Monimoy said, 'I became more suspicious when I heard her. I knew that my father must have kept the necklace in the drawer, because my mother had taken away the keys to the vault. So, I went quietly to the office room and opened all the drawers. I didn't find the box containing the necklace. Then I searched all the possible places where my father could have kept the box. It was nowhere. I was very nervous and so I woke up my father.'

Byomkesh lit another cigarette thoughtfully and looked at Rashamoy babu who again picked up the threads of his story, 'When we had no doubt that the necklace had gone, I suspected

Bhola. There was a Yale lock on my front door on the second floor—it is easy to go out from the inside, but impossible to access from the outside. The only one who was inside among the servants was Bhola. I had gone off to sleep; I didn't even know when Bhola went out. Maybe he left at about a quarter to twelve, took the necklace from the drawer and quietly went down the steps. Maybe he had an accomplice waiting outside, on the street.'

Byomkesh asked Monimoy, 'Did you see just one person?'

Monimoy said, 'Yes, there was no one else around.'

Byomkesh turned to his wife, 'And you?'

She said, 'I also saw only one person. I was looking down at the street for a long time, so I would have noticed a second person. But no, there was only one man.'

Byomkesh was quiet for some time, then he asked Rashamoy, 'Then what did you do?'

'Then the two of us talked about it and decided to inform the police. Moni went and stood at the main gate to prevent anyone from going out. The Officer in charge (OC) of the police station, Amaresh babu is well-known to me, and fortunately, he was there at that time. He came at once with two or three policemen.

'He first searched the first floor. All the servants, including Bhola, were sleeping. The police woke them up and searched them and their belongings thoroughly. But the necklace couldn't be found.

'Then Amaresh babu searched the second floor. He thought that the thief might have hidden it there for the timebeing and would remove it later when he would get a chance. But there was no sign of the necklace.

'Then Amaresh babu began questioning Bhola. He admitted that he had gone out. He said that at about eleven, when he found that I had gone off to sleep, he went down. All the other servants had gone off to sleep. He could not sleep, so he went down into the street for fresh air. He was not aware that Monimoy had not returned home. So, he quickly came in and went off to bed because the servants were given strict orders not to go out at night. This was his testimony. He said he knew nothing about the necklace.

'In the course of Amaresh babu's cross-questioning, it was found that Bhola has two brothers working in Calcutta—in Mechua Bazar. He is not very close to them. But when he had no other work on hand, he would sometimes visit them.

'While Amaresh babu was questioning Bhola, his policemen were searching the whole area outside the house—the sides of the street, the drains, the dustbin— and Moni was also there with them. But they got nothing. It was nearly daybreak. Amaresh babu kept one policeman on the second floor and left. He told Bhola before leaving that if he went out of the house, he would be arrested.

'Then as time passed, I became restless. I know that Amaresh babu is efficient and will try his best, but I just couldn't wait any longer. So I rang you up. Please help me recover my necklace— only you can do it, Byomkesh babu.'

Byomkesh smiled a little, 'You have a lot of confidence in me. I hope I will be able to fulfill your trust in me. Is Bhola at home?'

'Yes, he is in his room on the first floor.'

'I would like to ask him a few questions.'

Rashamoy babu looked at his son, 'Of course, Monimoy will call him for you.'

Bhola followed Monimoy into the room after a while. There was nothing distinctive in his appearance. His was a face which became thin and bony with age, leaving the jaw bones, nose and chin prominent. His body, too, was thin and wiry. He was about forty. There was no fear in his eyes but rather had an alert expression.

Byomkesh studied him for a minute or two and said, 'I want to ask you a few questions.'

Bhola said quite calmly, 'Yes, Sir.'

'Name?'

'Bhola Das.'

'Where is your original home?'

'Midnapur District.'

'How long have you been in Calcutta?'

'About fifteen years.'

'Do two of your brothers live in Calcutta?'

'Yes Sir, they stay together in a rented house in Mechua Bazar.'

'Why don't you stay with them?'

'I stay where I work.'

'Are you on good terms with your brothers?'

'It is okay, but my brothers are educated, I am not.'

'Where do they work?'

'My elder brother works at the post office and my second brother is in the Municipal Corporation.'

'Are you married?'

'Yes, I did marry but my wife is dead.'

'How long have you been working in this house?'

'For one and half years.'

'Where did you work before that?'

'In many places.'

'What work?'

'Massaging elderly people—I don't know any other work.'

He was intelligent enough to hide his true feelings even though he was not literate.

Byomkesh continued questioning, 'Everyone thinks that you have stolen the necklace!'

Bhola did not break down at this frontal attack. He did not show his anger either. He calmly denied, 'I have not even seen the diamond necklace.'

'When Monimoy babu gave the box containing the necklace to his father, you were in the room, but before he opened the box, he asked you to leave the room. You didn't guess anything even after that?'

'No, Sir.'

Byomkesh thought for some time with a frown on his forehead and then asked suddenly, 'Did you go out in the evening yesterday?'

At last, there was some sign of anxiety in Bhola's expression, 'Yes Sir, I went out in the evening for a short while to buy a towel. I asked my mistress to give me leave for some time.'

Byomkesh looked at Monimoy's wife—she nodded in agreement. Rashamoy babu's expression showed that he did not know about this. Even Monimoy was not in the know as he had already left the house to go to the club. But how did Byomkesh know that Bhola had stepped out of the house? Was it just conjecture?

He asked Bhola, 'How long did you stay out?'

'About an hour.'

'It took you one hour to buy a towel?'

'Sir, I roamed around a bit after buying the towel.'

'Did you meet anyone?'

'No.'

'Don't you have any friends?'

'I have a few acquaintances, but no friends.'

'Last night, after dinner, you were massaging Rashamoy babu's feet.'

'Yes, I do that every night.'

'For how long were you doing that?'

'I didn't see the time...till about eleven.'

'When you went to the first floor, were the other servants awake?'

'No, they were all asleep.'

'No one was awake?'

'No.'

'That's strange! What did you do then? Did you lie down?'

'Yes, Sir.'

'Then why did you go out at twelve?'

'I couldn't sleep for quite some time... So I thought if I got some fresh air, I would feel sleepy.'

'For how long did you stand outside?'

'Not more than three or four minutes. I did not know that Moni babu had not returned from the club. I saw him coming, so I quickly came in.'

'Did you shut the main door?'

'No, I saw him coming, so I didn't shut the door.'

Byomkesh looked the man up and down with an appreciative glance, then said, 'You may go now.'

After Bhola left, Rashamoy babu asked, 'What do you think?'

Byomkesh said disappointedly, 'A very careful person. But he admitted that he had gone out last evening.'

'What does it prove?'

'Nothing. But if he has any accomplice, he must have met the person before the theft; otherwise, how could the necklace vanish into thin air?'

'That's true!'

Our conversation was interrupted by a knock at the door. Monimoy got up, went to the door and brought in a big-build man in police uniform; no doubt he was Amaresh Mondal—the OC.'

He sat down and said, 'I went to Mechua Bazar and searched the house of Bhola's brothers, but...' Then his eyes landed on us—he stopped short.

Rashamoy babu said uneasily, 'Inspector Mondal, he is... er...Byomkesh Bakshi. You must have heard about him.'

Amaresh babu sat up straight and said joyfully, 'Who hasn't heard of Byomkesh Bakshi? I have heard about you from Promod Barat. Do you remember him? He worked with you in the Golap Colony case. He is my friend.'

Byomkesh smiled, 'Of course, I remember him! He is a very clever man.'

Amaresh babu said, 'He is a great fan of yours. So, you are also involved in this necklace case? It's my good fortune to be working with you! I heard from Promod that you are not interested in fame but only in seeking the truth.'

Byomkesh smiled meaningfully, 'Inspector Mondal, one never wants what one has—that's the way of the world. If there is any fame involved in this case, it will be yours only. I'll be happy to get my remuneration.'

Rashamoy babu said in a voice filled with emotion, 'Please don't call it remuneration, Byomkesh babu. It will be a gift of gratitude which you will deserve if I get back my necklace.'

Byomkesh turned to Amaresh babu, 'You have searched Bhola's brothers' house and got nothing?'

'No, nothing at all. His brothers had gone out to work. Their wives were at home. I searched the house thoroughly, but to no avail.'

Byomkesh said, 'So you think that Bhola has stolen the necklace with the help of his brothers?'

Amaresh babu said, 'He may have other accomplices besides

his brothers, but there must have been an accomplice for sure. Otherwise, how did the necklace vanish?'

'But Monimoy babu and his wife did not see anyone else but one man.'

'Maybe, before they noticed Bhola, someone else had come and taken the box from him.'

'But Monimoy babu's wife was looking down at the street for a long time. Wouldn't she have noticed another man?'

'Then you don't think Bhola was involved?'

'I don't know. You have done everything that was needed. Now, we have to just think.' Byomkesh got up, 'We will leave now; if I think of a solution, I'll let you know.'

∽

After returning home, I asked Byomkesh, 'Who do you suspect?'

Byomkesh said, 'I suspect three of them.'

Startled, I asked, 'Who are the three?'

'Bhola, Monimoy and Monimoy's wife…'

Saying this, he went off to bathe. I started thinking… Yes all three could be suspected. A wealthy man's son is always in need of money. Monimoy must be playing cards at high stakes in the club that he visits. Maybe he was in debt and was frightened of telling his father, and so…!

And Monimoy's wife… The girl was quiet by nature but the expression of anxiety on her face was quite apparent. She could be helping her husband or may have removed the box at a moment of temptation.

But how could whoever that stole the necklace remove it without a trace?

Byomkesh spent the whole afternoon staring at the ceiling and uttering not a single word. After a cup of tea in the afternoon, he said suddenly, 'Let's go out.'

The Vanishing Trick

'Where?'

'Let's go and have a look at the pavement in front of Rashamoy babu's house. I haven't seen the place properly.'

It took us about twenty minutes to walk to Rashamoy babu's house. On reaching the place, Byomkesh began looking around. The shops on either side of the door were open—a shop of homeopathic medicine, a watch shop and two cloth shops. All the shops were full of buyers. The footpath was crowded as well.

The second floor of Rashamoy babu's house had about four windows overlooking the street. Monimoy's wife was looking down at the street through one of those windows. I was looking up. Then I looked down to see that Byomkesh was staring at the main door of Rashamoy babu's house. I saw that the door was open and Monimoy had come out to post a letter.

Byomkesh called out to him, 'Monimoy babu, who did you write to?'

Monimoy was startled at Byomkesh's voice and turned around. Seeing us, he said, 'What are you doing here now? Any news?'

Byomkesh said, 'I'll give you my news later. Who did you write to?'

Monimoy said, a bit sadly, 'I gave the bad news to my mother. I asked her to return home quickly. But the letter won't go today. The box has already been cleared. The next clearance is early tomorrow morning. But you must have some good news for us, please tell me.'

Byomkesh said, 'When I came out of my house, I had no news for you, but now I have some good news!'

'What news? Where is the necklace? Do you know?'

'Yes, I do. But I'll talk to you about it later. Now, I have to go for some important work.'

'My father is eager to get some news from you, please come upstairs for some time.'

Byomkesh said, 'No, I've to finish my work first. Ajit will come upstairs with you. Tell Rashamoy babu that he will get his necklace by tomorrow morning.' Saying this, Byomkesh walked away quickly.

I went up with Monimoy.

Rashamoy babu kept on asking me, 'Will I really get my necklace back?'

I said, 'I have never known Byomkesh to give false assurance. Since he has given you his word, I am sure you'll get it back.'

Then I had tea, cakes and expensive cigarettes, and returned home in their Cadillac.

5

It was past evening, but Byomkesh had not yet returned. He came back after about an hour. I asked, 'Where did you go?'

'I had some business with Amaresh babu at the police station.'

'What business?'

'Important business. You go to sleep now. We have to get up early tomorrow morning.'

I knew that he wouldn't answer my questions.

I had my dinner with a glum expression. Noticing that, Satyabati asked, 'Why are you annoyed?'

'Your husband is a tortoise.'

Satyabati laughed, 'Why a tortoise of all animals?'

'A tortoise doesn't communicate but withdraws into its shell.'

Satyabati was very sympathetic, 'You are right. Why can't he understand our curiosity?'

Early in the morning, Byomkesh pushed me awake, 'Get up, Ajit, we have to go out right now.'

We went out immediately. The street lights were still on. After walking for some time, I realized that we were heading towards Rashamoy babu's house.

'What do you want with Rashamoy babu this early in the morning?'

'I have no business with him.'

'Then why are we out so early?'

'There was an urgent need. You must wait to see my masterstroke; the climax is always at the end.'

'Why are you talking in riddles?' I was quite annoyed.

Byomkesh grinned, 'I want to be around when the postbox near Rashamoy babu's house is cleared in the morning today.'

A few bulbs lighted up in my head, but the darkness was not dispelled completely.

When we reached the house, we found two men standing there in the shadow inconspicuously. Byomkesh spoke to them in a whisper. Then we stood at the crossroads in such a way that we were not directly visible.

I looked at my wristwatch—it was still ten minutes to five. There was still no one on the streets, a few trucks full of vegetables were moving in different directions. Rashamoy babu's house was enveloped in darkness. The lamp post opposite the street threw its light on the main door. Next to the door was the postbox. It was not easily noticeable as it was covered with handbills of different varieties.

The minutes were passing slowly. I could feel the passing of each minute with my heartbeat. It was five now. My nerves and muscles were taut with excitement.

When a man suddenly appeared in front of the postbox, I was totally unprepared. It seemed like a ghostly appearance. He was wearing a khaki uniform and had two large bags on his shoulders. He kept the bags on the footpath, took out a bunch of keys from his pocket and started opening the postbox.

Byomkesh waved his hand to indicate that we must close in. I found that there were others besides the two plain-clothed policemen whom we had seen.

As soon as the man opened the door of the postbox, we surrounded him. He turned around with a fright. Then seeing the eight of us, he said in a trembling voice, 'Who are you? What do you want?'

Byomkesh asked in a stern voice, 'You are Bhutnath Das—Bhola's elder brother?'

Bhutnath Das's thin face contorted with fright and his eyes bulged out. He said in a trembling voice, 'Who…who are you?'

Amaresh babu bellowed, 'We are the police!'

I had not noticed earlier that Amaresh babu was also in the group. He came forward and clasped Bhutnath's shoulder. I felt that it was an attempt to scare Bhutnath. It yielded the desired result. Bhutnath howled with fear, 'Bhola! You have ruined me. I'll lose my job and will have to go to jail!'

As soon as he stopped, Amaresh babu said, 'Where have you kept the stolen necklace? Take it out at once!'

Bhutnath fell at Amaresh babu's feet, 'Sir! I have not touched it with my hands—it is still inside the postbox.'

We were all a little startled. The necklace was in that nondescript postbox as described from the night before last when it was stolen from Rashamoy babu's house!

Amaresh babu roared, 'Take it out!'

Bhutnath turned to the postbox. He put his hand in and pulled out a box from behind a pile of letters. It was wrapped in a cloth that was stitched around. There was no doubt that it contained the necklace. Bhutnath handed it to Amaresh babu and cried, 'Take it, Sir. God knows I have not seen what is inside the box.'

Just at that time, Rashamoy babu's door opened and the old man walked out to us with the help of a stick. His son and his daughter-in-law followed him.

'Amaresh babu! Byomkesh babu! My necklace?' There was astonishment in his slumberous eyes.

Byomkesh handed him the box, 'This is your necklace—please open it and check.'

∽

At about nine-thirty in the morning, we were back in our house, sitting opposite each other. Satyabati had served a second cup of tea and we were doing a post-mortem on the case of the stolen necklace.

Byomkesh said, 'It was a waste of time. If I had noticed earlier that the postbox was right next to the main door of the house, the case would have been solved in five minutes. This city is full of postboxes of this kind that escape notice because they are covered with all kinds of handbills. It is not a problem for those who know of their existence; but for those who do not, they are difficult to locate.

'At first, I suspected three people—Bhola, Monimoy and his wife. I was certain that one of them was the thief or it could be that two of the three had worked together. It could be Monimoy and Bhola, or Monimoy and his wife.

'But how was the stolen good hidden so fast, and so well at that? As we know, within an hour or so of the theft, the police were informed. No one went out of the house. The police came and searched the house and its neighbourhood thoroughly—nothing could be found. If Bhola was the culprit... He had gone out into the street but had not met anyone. So, what did he do with the necklace? The same question applies to Monimoy and his wife.

'But, of course, the main suspect was Bhola. When Monimoy gave the box to his father, Bhola was present in the room. It was easy for him to assume that this was an expensive ornament in the box. Then he had gone out to buy a towel. He could have contacted his accomplice then. But how and when did he give the necklace to his accomplice—that was the mystery.'

Satyabati came in at that moment and commented, 'So the tortoise is talking!'

Byomkesh glared at her—I realized that he was not at all pleased to be compared with a tortoise! I made a mental note to use this simile to tease him in the future. After a bit of silence, he began, 'The more I observed and thought about the family, I began to realize that Monimoy and his wife could be excluded from the list of suspects. Rashamoy babu was an affectionate father who would not hesitate to help Monimoy with money if he ever needed it. The same went for his daughter-in-law. They would not have to steal something from him that they would have gotten if they only asked for.

'Bhola had both the opportunity and the motive. He was a cool customer. He had probably taken up the job with a rich jeweller with the ulterior motive of stealing. He got his chance. An expensive ornament was brought into the house and the mistress had gone off with the keys to the vault!

'Bhola's accomplice was his eldest brother, Bhutnath. It was a good connection. His job was to collect letters from the postboxes of this area, three times a day.

'Bhola met his brother after he had gone out to buy the towel. He told Bhutnath that if he found a small box while clearing the postbox next to Rashamoy babu's main door the next morning, he was not to touch it but leave it there. Bhutnath is a simple and honest person, but he succumbed to the temptation. Bhola must have promised him a hefty amount! Poor fellow, he will not only lose his government job but may be arrested too.

'As soon as I found Monimoy posting a letter in the postbox last evening, everything became clear to me. Bhola had told me that one of his brothers worked in the post office. Bhola went out in the middle of the night and slipped the box into the postbox and came up again. So no other person was seen near the house. Of course, he did not know that Monimoy had not returned from the club and that his wife was standing—waiting for him—looking out the window.

'When I realized everything, I went straight to Amaresh babu. I enquired from the post office to find out what job Bhola's brother did there. What was left to do was to get a confession from the culprit by setting a trap, and that is what we did this morning.'

There was a knock at the door. Monimoy was standing there. He said smilingly, 'My father has sent me.'

He took out a small, velvet box from his pocket, placed it in front of Byomkesh and said, 'My father has asked me to request you to accept this. He couldn't come himself because of his ailment.'

'There is no need... He has an able son to do these jobs for him. Is he happy to get his necklace back?'

'Of course! He told me to tell you that this small gift is not worth you or your work but you must accept it.'

'Let's see what it is!' Byomkesh opened the box. It was a beautiful diamond ring!

Byomkesh looked at it admiringly, 'Please tell your father that I am not worth this ring. Please have a cup of tea.'

'No, I'll come another day. I have to leave for Delhi by the evening flight.'

Monimoy left. Satyabati, who must have been eavesdropping, entered the room at once. Before Byomkesh could hide the box, she snatched it away. 'You are not worth it but I am!' she said, and ran inside. Byomkesh heaved a sigh of disappointment!

6

The Bloodline
Rakter Daag

It was the first spring since our country gained independence. The southern breeze was blowing pleasantly and the trees in Calcutta were in full bloom. It is said that this season brings fresh energy and vigour in people.

Byomkesh was relaxing on the divan, reading a book of poems. I was ruminating on the swiftness with which time flies and how the evening of my life was fast approaching. The advent of spring in recent years always brought this sad feeling to my mind—I was growing old.

Satyabati entered the room in the evening. I noticed that she had done up her hair and adorned it with flowers. She was wearing a light yellow coloured saree. It was after a long time that she had taken such care to dress up. She sat next to Byomkesh and said, 'What are you reading all day? Let's go out!'

Byomkesh did not reply. I asked, 'Where will you go? To the Maidan?'

Satyabati said, 'No! No! Outside Calcutta, maybe to Kashmir, or…'

Byomkesh sat up, and with a finger in his book, said dramatically, 'How I wish to fly to distant horizons, but where are the means? My feet are chained, but my heart is soaring!'

Surprised, I exclaimed, 'Are you quoting from somewhere?'

Byomkesh said mysteriously, 'Why should I tell you?'

He lay down with his book again. When one had no work, one often immersed themselves in activities they had previously no interest in. Byomkesh had started reading poems and threatened me that he would become an expert in modern verse. I was scared that he might even start writing poems of his own, seeing as anyone could write modern poems, as they rarely had any rhyme or reason! The vision of the great truth seeker Byomkesh turning into 'Byomkesh, the poet' made me shiver with fright!

Satyabati pinched his toe and said, 'Get up! Why are you ignoring what I just said?'

Byomkesh sat up with a start, 'Do you know how much it costs to go to Kashmir?'

'How much?'

'A few thousand! Where will I get that kind of money?'

Satyabati got up angrily. 'I don't know all that. Are we going or not?'

'I am telling you, I have no money.'

Just at that moment, there was a knock at the door. I was disappointed at losing the chance of witnessing a marital quarrel! Satyabati quickly went out of the room, after throwing an angry glance at Byomkesh.

I switched on the light and opened the door. The person who stood outside looked like a young boy at the first glance. He was slightly built and fair, not very tall and with the faint trace of a moustache above his upper lip. He was very well-dressed—his clothes and his leather shoes looked pretty expensive.

'Who are you looking for?'

'The truth seeker, Byomkesh Bakshi.'

'Come in,' I stood aside for him to enter. Now I observed him under the strong electric light in the room. He was not as young as he looked. His eyes had the sharpness of experience—there were dark circles under them. The veneer of youthfulness couldn't completely screen the harshness of age. But even then, I was certain that he was not more than twenty-five years of age.

Byomkesh was sitting on the divan and observing our visitor. He then stood up, asked him to sit and sat down after him. 'What do you want me to do for you?'

The young man did not answer at once but sat down and looked at Byomkesh thoroughly for some time and said, 'Yes, you will serve my purpose.'

Byomkesh raised his eyebrows indignantly and said, 'Really? What will be your purpose?'

The young man took out bundles of notes from his pocket and threw them carelessly on the table, 'If I die suddenly, you will investigate the cause of my death. I'll naturally not be able to pay you later, so I am making your payment in advance. There are a few thousand there. Please count the money.'

Byomkesh picked the currency notes, counted them and kept them aside. He looked up at me; I found his eyes dancing with amusement! Then he looked sternly at the young man and said, 'I'll ask you a few questions, and I'll decide whether I'll take up your case or not after hearing your answers.'

The young man opened a gold cigarette case and offered one to Byomkesh. When Byomkesh refused, he lighted one himself, blew out the smoke and said, 'Ask, but I may not answer all your questions.'

Byomkesh was silent for some time. Then he asked casually, 'What is your name?'

The young man smiled—it was an attractive smile. He said, 'Oh, yes! I have not introduced myself. My name is Satyakam Das.'

'Are you giving me a false name?'

'No.'

'Where do you stay?'

'33/34, Amherst Street.'

'What do you do?'

'Nothing much. Have you heard of the Das Choudhury Company's Suchitra Emporium?'

'Yes, the huge departmental store at Esplanade.'

'I am a partner of the store.'

'Who is the other partner?'

There was a sharp intake of breath before Satyakam said, 'My father, Ushapati Das.'

Byomkesh looked at him questioningly. Satyakam hesitated for a minute and then said unwillingly, 'My maternal grandfather had started the Emporium. Then my father became a partner. My grandfather is now dead; he willed his portion to me. My mother was the only child of my grandfather. I am also the only child of my mother.'

'I understand,' Byomkesh was silent for some time. Then he said in a disinterested voice, 'Do you drink?'

Satyakam was not a bit embarrassed, 'Yes, did you smell it on me?'

'How old are you?'

'I am twenty-one. Do you want to know my date of birth? It is 14 July 1927.' Satyakam gave us a mocking smile.

'How long have you been drinking?'

'Since I was fourteen,' Satyakam lighted another cigarette from the butt of the finished one.

'Do you drink all the time?'

'I drink whenever I want to.' Satyakam pulled out a small flask containing alcohol from his pocket.

Byomkesh sat quietly for some time. I was nonplussed. What a shameless fellow!

Byomkesh looked up again and asked in a quiet voice, 'Do you suffer from other allied faults of character?'

Satyakam grinned, 'Why are you calling these faults when most people indulge in them?'

I felt sick, but Byomkesh was unperturbed.

'Let's not philosophize on such elevated subjects. Do you lust after girls from respectable families too?'

'Yes!' The man sounded satisfied with his reply.

'How many girls have you ruined so far?'

'I have lost count, Byomkesh babu.' He smiled shamelessly.

Byomkesh looked at him distastefully, 'You are saying that you may die suddenly. Do you fear that someone might murder you?'

'Yes.'

'Who do you suspect—the relatives of the girls you have ruined? Or anyone else?'

'I do suspect someone, but I'll not reveal the name to you.'

'Won't you try to save yourself?'

Satyakam made a helpless gesture with his hands, 'No use trying, Byomkesh babu. I'll leave now. I have an appointment tonight.'

It was easy to understand that it was not a business appointment from the way he smiled.

When he reached the door, Byomkesh asked, 'How shall I know when you are murdered?'

He turned around, 'You will hear it in the newspapers. I don't think you will have to wait very long.'

I closed the door after Satyakam had left. Satyabati entered with a smiling face; she must have been close by.

'You were worried about money—now you have got it!'

Byomkesh gave the money to Satyabati, 'Yes my dear, you will enjoy the fruit of my labour. So start preparing for your Kashmir trip!'

He looked at me and said, 'How did you find the fellow?'

'I have never met such a shameless creature in my life!'

Byomkesh said, 'But isn't it strange that he doesn't want to save himself from being murdered but only wants his murder to be investigated?'

༄

The next morning, Satyabati said, 'How can we go to Kashmir without warm clothes and proper bedding?'

Byomkesh said, 'But we have the quilts that we used in Patna last winter!'

Satyabati said, 'Those were my brother's. The few we have are only enough for the Calcutta winter. We need two good blankets, and I need an overcoat for myself.'

'Ajit, let's go out.'

I asked, 'Where?'

'To Suchitra Emporium; we will do both jobs at the same time.'

I said, 'Let Satyabati come with us. She can choose whatever she wants.'

But Satyabati was reluctant to go as she was busy with housework.

Byomkesh said, 'I'll choose the blankets and bring them for her. I am sure she will like them.'

Satyabati smiled sweetly. Normally, she would have asked me to choose, because she had more confidence in my choice than his; but, of course, this was the season of spring and love was in the air!

When we reached the Emporium at Esplanade at about nine-thirty, we found that the shutters and the doors of the shop had just been opened. It was a huge shop, with large glass doors and glass showcases. Some customers were already there, most of them being sharply dressed upper-class women. An elderly man was walking up and down the length and breadth of the shop to keep an eye on the salespeople.

As soon as we entered, he approached us and politely asked us what we wanted.

Byomkesh looked awkwardly and said, 'A couple of blankets, do you have them?'

'Yes, of course. Please follow me. Anything else?'

'And a lady's overcoat.'

'Please take the lift and go upstairs. You will find both the blankets and the overcoat there.'

As we stood in front of the lift, we heard a voice behind us, 'I'll look after these gentlemen.'

We turned to find that it was Satyakam. He was dressed impeccably in a silk suit.

The elderly gentleman said, 'They are looking for blankets and a ladies overcoat. Take them upstairs.' He smiled slightly at us and went off in another direction.

Byomkesh looked at the gentleman pointedly and asked Satyakam, 'He is?'

'My partner.' Satyakam gave a crooked smile.

'That is, your father.'

'Yes.'

Now I observed the elderly gentleman. He was speaking with another client but was glancing uneasily at our direction. He was about forty-five. His hair had a touch of grey. He was stockily built and somehow looked like an ascetic. He was probably a strict and self-controlled person, as he did not seem very sweet-tempered.

We went upstairs in the lift.

Satyakam looked at Byomkesh with amusement and said, 'Are you really going to buy something or is it just an excuse to come here to investigate?'

'We do wish to buy some things.'

This floor was not as well-decorated as the ground floor. It was something like a storage space. Even then, a few customers were moving around. Satyakam asked the salesman to show us a few different kinds of blankets. In truth, Byomkesh was ignorant about these things. So I did the choosing.

Next was the overcoat. They were very expensive. As we were looking, Satyakam said, 'Don't worry about the size; overcoats can be a bit loose. If it is too big, come back to me and I will get it changed.'

I chose a coat, but when I saw the price tag, I pushed it away. Satyakam understood, 'Don't worry about the price; it is for the other customers, not for you. You will get it at the cost price.'

He took us to the cashier and said, 'Please bill all these items at cost price.'

'All right,' said the elderly cashier. I looked at the cash memo and found that it was nearly half the price marked on the tags. I was very happy. I began to change my earlier opinion of Satyakam.

Just at that moment, a young lady came in. She was a well-dressed, attractive girl. Satyakam glanced at her and his expression changed like magic, in just a second. He looked at us distractedly and said, 'I think you have finished; I'll leave you now.'

The bee flew straight to the rose. When we came out of the shop, we turned to see that the young lady was listening to Satyakam with rapt attention.

We came home and showed our purchases to Satyabati, who praised Byomkesh for his choice. This was the spirit of spring!

When I told her how Satyakam had reduced the price of the things, she was all praises for him, 'What a good boy he is!'

Byomkesh said skeptically, 'Yes, he is such a good boy. If he remains so good to his customers, the shop will close down even before he is murdered!'

We went out in the evening. This time, our destination was 33/34, Amherst Street. The house had a small iron gate, after which a narrow pathway led to the front door. It was a two-storeyed house and did not seem too large from the front. Next to the main door were two windows. On top of the windows were two small, circular balconies. The inside of the house was still dark, as the lights had yet to be switched on. It seemed, in the fading light of the evening, that a lady was on one of the balconies, either stitching or reading a book. She was faintly visible through the iron railings of the balcony.

'Byomkesh babu!'

Startled, we turned back to find a man whom we had earlier seen walking on the pavement, calling for us. He was a well-built man, with cropped hair. His face seemed familiar.

The man said, 'Sir, don't you recognize me? I came to collect the donation for Saraswati Puja from your house the other day. I stay in your area. My name is Nanda Ghosh.'

Byomkesh said, 'Oh, yes, yes. But what are you doing in this area at this time of the day, that too wrapped in a shawl?'

'Sir.' Nanda took out his right hand from under his shawl for a second. We saw a short, strong baton in his hand.

Byomkesh looked at him suspiciously and asked, 'What are you up to?'

'I will tell you, Sir,' he came near Byomkesh and said in a whisper, 'A fellow lives in this house; I am going to bash him up.'

'Really, but why?'

'I have a reason to, Sir. But, what are you doing here? Do you know anyone in this house?'

'We know Satyakam. You want to beat him up, I suppose?'

'Yes,' Nanda became a bit upset. 'Do you know him well?'

'No, but I want to know why you want to beat him. Has he harmed you in any way?'

'Harm? It is a long story, Sir. Please come with me. We have a bodybuilding club nearby. I will tell you everything there.'

'Let's go.'

We followed Nanda into a walled space with a few dilapidated rooms. In the open space, a few shorts-clad young men were doing physical exercises of different kinds. Nanda took us to one of the rooms.

There was a mat spread out on the floor, and sitting in the middle of it was the instructor of these young men. We came to know later that he was the proprietor of the club as well. The gentleman's name was Bhuteshwar Baag. The name suited him to perfection—not only was his complexion as pale as that of a ghost (*bhut*), but also his face was as big and as ferocious as that of a tiger (*baag*). Moreover, his physique could put an elephant to shame. He was about sixty years old without a single strand of hair on his head. He must have been a wrestler in his youth. It seemed to me that as he grew old, he opened this club.

Nanda said, 'Bhuteshwar da, Byomkesh babu is a very famous detective; he knows Satyakam.'

Bhuteshwar glanced at Byomkesh and said, 'Are you from the police force? Are you here to protect that chap?'

Byomkesh replied with great humility that he had nothing to do with the police. He further added that he did not know Satyakam well. He only wished to know why Satyakam had to be beaten up.

Now Bhuteshwar was pacified, 'That fellow is a rascal. A few gentlemen from this area have complained about him. He has been troubling their daughters. I will not allow this to happen in my area.'

Just then, a few more sweating wrestlers came into the room and surrounded us. It was obvious that the idea of beating up Satyakam was supported by all. I became quite nervous. Would they take out their ire against Satyakam on us?

But Byomkesh saved the situation. He said in a calm voice, 'If a person in the area has been misbehaving, it is the moral right and duty of the people of the area to teach him a lesson. As far as I am concerned, I know that Satyakam needs to be taught a lesson. But see to it that you don't get involved in a murder, and do the work carefully so that you don't get caught by the police.'

Nanda smiled with relief, 'That's why I have offered to do the job. I don't belong to this area. I'll beat him up and get out of this place. No one will be able to identify me, even if they see me beating him up.'

Byomkesh said with a smile, 'Even then, if there is any trouble, please inform me. Goodbye, Bhuteshwar babu.'

Nanda accompanied us to the main street and then went back. Byomkesh heaved a sigh of relief, 'We have come back safely from the tiger's den, thank God!'

I said, 'But you should not have encouraged them to beat up Satyakam. You have taken his money.'

Byomkesh said, 'But by just getting beaten up, he might escape death. Won't that be better for him?'

∽

Although I have never worked in an office, I invariably get up late on Sundays. I must have inherited the tendency from my forefathers who had been regular office-goers.

I woke up late, at about seven-thirty in the morning, and sleepily stepped into the drawing room. Byomkesh was reading the newspaper intently. He heard me coming in but did not lift his eyes from the paper and said, as if addressing the paper itself, 'Is this a vision that I see before me?'

I said suspiciously, 'What's happened?'

He put away the paper and said, 'Satyakam died last night. '

I was startled, 'How? When?'

'I don't know. We have to reach there within half an hour.'

I picked up the paper to read the news; it took up about five lines at the bottom of the page.

Last night, the owner of the well-known Suchitra Emporium, Satyakam Das, died under mysterious circumstances. The police are investigating the case.

So, Satyakam did foresee his death, after all! But did he think it would happen so soon? The first thing that came to my mind was the picture of Nanda Ghosh, hiding a strong baton under his shawl and moving around suspiciously near Satyakam's house last evening.

We reached Amherst Street at about eight-thirty. A constable was standing in front of the house. After a little hesitation, he allowed us to go in.

We walked along the brick-laid pathway and reached the front door, which was already open. But we saw no one there. We heard no sound of weeping from inside the house. Byomkesh stood stock-still as he reached the front door. He pointed to the ground and I noticed that there was a large, dried up patch of bloodstain in front of the door, just where the path had ended.

We exchanged glances. Byomkesh nodded his head and we walked to the front door, avoiding the stain. There were two doors on the wide verandah—one door had a lock hanging from it while the other door was open. Through the door, we could see a medium-sized office room. Ushapati Das was sitting alone in front of a large table. He had two elbows on the table, with his chin resting on his hands. As we walked in, he looked at us with a glazed, terror-stricken expression. Then he asked in a blank voice, 'What do you want?'

Byomkesh stood by the table and said sympathetically, 'We are extremely sorry that we are disturbing you at this time. My name is Byomkesh Bakshi.'

Ushapati became slightly more alert and looked at us, his eyes darting from one face to the other. He said, 'Where have I seen you before? In Suchitra, I think. What did you say your name was?'

'Byomkesh Bakshi, and this is my friend Ajit Banerjee. We came to your shop yesterday.'

It did not seem that Ushapati had ever heard our names before. But his business instincts were sharp and his inherent politeness to his clients controlled his emotions. He said in a quiet tone, 'Do you need anything? I am a bit preoccupied. There has been a mishap in the house.'

Byomkesh said, 'I know, that is why we have come. About Satyakam babu.'

'Did you know Satyakam?'

'We met him only the day before yesterday. He had come to me with a proposal.'

'What proposal?'

'He asked me to investigate if he should suddenly die an unnatural death.'

This time, Ushapati sat up. He gazed at us intently for a long while then, as if controlling his emotions with great effort. He said, 'Please sit down. So Satyakam had guessed that something was going to happen to him soon. But please pardon me, why did Satyakam go to you? What do you do? Do you belong to the police department? But the police came last night already.'

'No, I have nothing to do with the police. I am a truth

seeker—you could say a private detective.'

'Oh! Who did Satyakam suspect? Did he tell you that?'

'No, he did not name anyone. If you give us permission, we can start investigating.'

'But the police have already taken up the case. What more can you do?'

'I can't say whether we'll be at all successful, but we can try.'

It was obvious that Ushapati had not lost his business sense despite the shock of losing his only son. 'You are a private detective; what are your fees?'

Byomkesh said, 'You don't have to give me anything at all. Satyakam babu already paid me in advance.'

Ushapati looked at Byomkesh sharply, 'I see. If you want to investigate, you can do so, but it is of no use.'

'Why is it of no use?'

'Satyakam won't come back to us, no matter what we do now. We'll be digging up some old skeletons unnecessarily.'

Byomkesh stared at Ushapati for some time and said in a quiet voice, 'I can well understand what is going on in your mind. Please, rest assured, I'll not expose any skeletons in the family cupboard; my work is just to find out the truth.'

Ushapati heaved a tired sigh, 'All right, what do I have to do?'

'Please tell us how and when the death occurred.'

Ushapati looked more disturbed than ever. He pressed his hands on his chest once and said, 'Yes, I'll have to tell you everything. Who else will do that? I was sleeping in my room last night when I was woken up by a noise at about one o'clock. It was a loud thud, and it came from the front door.'

'Excuse me, which room do you sleep in?'

'Just above this room. The next room is my wife's.'

'Where did Satyakam sleep?'

'He slept downstairs. The room which is locked was his.

My wife's room is just above it.'

'Why did Satyakam babu sleep downstairs?'

Instead of answering the question, Ushapati looked distractedly out the window. It was obvious from his expression that Satyakam slept downstairs so that he could move freely in and out of the house at any hour of the day and night, especially since he always returned home late at night.

At that moment, a young girl entered the room with a glass of juice for Ushapati. As soon as she saw us, she said, 'Uncle.' and stood at the door undecidedly. She was about eighteen or nineteen, well-built and attractive. Right then, she looked nervous.

Ushapati turned towards her and said, 'Please take it away.' The girl left the room.

Byomkesh asked, 'Who are the other people in your house?'

Ushapati said, 'Besides us, my nephew and niece.'

'Was she your niece?'

'Yes.'

'How long have they been staying with you?'

'A year ago, their father died. Their mother had died earlier. I am looking after them now.'

'What about the servants?'

'We have an old servant, Sahadeb; besides him, there are a maid and a cook, but they don't stay at night.'

'Tell us about last night.'

Ushapati rubbed his eyes with his palms and said, 'Yes, I heard a sound and came out to the balcony. It was dark below and I could not see anything. Then I heard Sahadeb shouting from the front door below. I rushed downstairs when I saw that Sahadeb was standing in front of the open main door, and Satyakam was lying dead just outside the door. The bullet had pierced his back.'

'Bullet? From a gun?'

'Yes. Satyakam always came home late. Sahadeb slept in the closed passage downstairs and opened the main door as soon he heard Satyakam's knock. But last night, he did not hear any knock. Satyakam was shot from the back even before he could knock.'

Byomkesh exclaimed, 'Bullet! I had thought... Anyway please continue.'

Ushapati heaved a sigh, 'Next... What else? I rang up the police.'

Byomkesh thought for a while, and then he asked, 'Who locked Satyakam's room?'

Ushapati said, 'Whenever Satyakam went out, he would lock his room and keep the keys with himself. He must have locked his room yesterday too.'

'So the police must have taken the keys.'

'Most probably.'

'Did the police not open his room?'

'No.'

'I have nothing more to ask you, but could I meet and talk to the other members of the house?'

'All right, who do you wish to talk to?'

'Is Sahadeb at home?'

'Must be. I'll call him.'

Ushapati got up, called Sahadeb from the door and came back to sit down again.

Sahadeb entered the room. He was a very old man—just skin and bones; his hair and even his eyebrows were grey. His eyes had a vacant look.

Byomkesh asked, 'You are Sahadeb, correct? For how many years have you been working in this house?'

Sahadeb did not answer, but stared at us blankly.

Ushapati said, 'He has been working here from the time of my father-in-law for about thirty-five years.'

Byomkesh said, 'Last night, you...'

Before he could complete, Sahadeb said with folded hands, 'Sir, I don't know anything.'

Byomkesh said, 'Listen to me first, then answer. When Satyakam babu knocked at the door last night, were you awake?'

Sahadeb repeated, 'I don't know anything.'

Byomkesh looked at him sharply, 'Try to remember. Did you hear a sound?'

'I don't know anything.'

All the questions that Byomkesh asked elicited the same blank response, 'Sir, I don't know anything.'

It was impossible to fathom whether Sahadeb knew anything or not, but one thing was obvious—he would not say a word even if he knew something.

Byomkesh looked irritated, 'You may go. Ushapati babu, could you please call your niece?'

'Sahadeb, call Chumki.'

Sahadeb left the room. Chumki entered after a while. She tried to stand firmly next to the table. She was looking a bit more nervous than before. She glanced at us and looked down quickly.

Byomkesh said, 'You have been staying in this house since last year, your uncle has told us. Where did you stay before that?'

Chumki answered in a half-whisper, 'Maniktala.'

'Do you study?'

'Yes, in college.'

'Your brother?'

'He studies in college too.'

'When did you get to know about this mishap last night?'

Chumki took a deep breath and said slowly, 'I was sleeping.

My brother banged at my door and I woke up.'

'Do you bolt your door from inside before sleeping?'

Chumki seemed taken aback. 'Yes,' she stammered.

'Where is your bedroom?'

'Downstairs, at the back of the house, next to my brother's.'

'But you did not hear the gunshot?'

'No!'

'What did you do after getting up?'

'My brother and I came to this room. I found my uncle ringing up the police.'

'And your aunt?'

'I did not see her then. I went upstairs from here and found that she had fainted on the floor.' Chumki's eyes filled with tears.

Byomkesh said gently, 'Now you can go. Please send your brother.'

Her brother entered as soon as she left. It seemed that he was waiting just outside.

The brother and the sister looked alike. But the brother had a strange way of staring unblinkingly, like an owl. He stood next to the table and stared at us. Byomkesh started his cross-questioning.

'What's your name?'

'Shitangsu Dutta.'

'Age?'

'Twenty.'

'Were you awake last night?'

'Yes.'

'What were you doing, studying?'

'Yes.'

'Studying for examinations?'

'No, Gorky's *The Lower Depths*. It is my habit to read at night.'

'Did you hear the gunshot?'

'Yes, but I did not realize that it was a gunshot.'

'Then?'

'I went only when I heard Sahadeb da shouting.'

'Then you came back and woke up your sister?'

'Yes.'

Byomkesh was silent for some time.

I glanced at Ushapati. He seemed to be immersed in the depths of his own thoughts. He was not listening to the conversation.

Byomkesh renewed his questions, 'Do you also bolt your room when you sleep?'

'No.'

'But Chumki does.'

'She is a girl.'

'Did you go out of the house after everyone retired last night?'

'No.'

'Is there any other door to go out of the house besides the front door?'

'Yes, there is a back door.'

'Did anyone go out of the back door last night?'

'No, I would have heard it if anyone did go out. The back door is just next to my room, and it makes a noise when opened. Besides, the back door is always locked.'

'Really? Who has the keys?'

'Sahadeb da.'

'Did you know that Satyakam babu was always late in returning home?'

'Yes.'

'Did you know when he came back every night?'

'Not every night, but sometimes.'

'All right, you may go now.'

Shitangsu stared at Byomkesh for sometime and then left the room.

Byomkesh then looked at Ushapati and asked hesitantly, 'Could we meet your wife?'

Ushapati was startled, 'My wife...but in this condition?'

'I understand. She doesn't have to come here. I'll go to her and ask...'

His sentence remained incomplete as a lady entered the room impatiently. It was obvious that she was Ushapati's wife. She said to us sharply, 'Why are you bothering my husband? Who are you? What do you want?'

We stood up quickly. The lady was about forty years old but looked younger. She was fair and still beautiful. Right then, she was more annoyed than sad at the loss of her only son.

Byomkesh said humbly, 'Please forgive me. I am doing my duty.'

The lady said, 'Who has called you? You have no duty here. Go away and don't disturb us.'

Byomkesh said, 'Don't you want the mystery of the death of your son to be solved?'

'No, please go away and leave us in peace.'

We looked at Ushapati. He looked startled, as if he could not believe his eyes and ears. He was staring at his wife, as if he was seeing her for the first time in his life!

'All right, we'll go.'

She glanced at him and went out of the room.

∽

We came out of the main door. Ushapati followed us, the expression of surprise still lingering on his face. Before closing the door, he said, 'Please think of our mental turmoil and try to forgive our behaviour.'

The door was nearly closing when Byomkesh said, 'What's that?'

We had not noticed it when we came in. On the outside of the main door, about a foot above the threshold, a tinsel disc was stuck with gum on the door. Byomkesh bent down and felt it with his finger.

'It is a disc made with golden paper and stuck on the door with gum. What is it?'

Ushapati said hesitantly, 'I don't know. This is the first time I am noticing it.'

Byomkesh said, 'It has been stuck on recently. One could understand if there were small children in the house, but could you please enquire?'

Ushapati called Sahadeb, but his response was the usual, 'I don't know anything.'

Shitangsu said, 'When I returned home last evening, it wasn't there.'

My head was buzzing with a plethora of thoughts. Did the murderer leave his signature in this way as they always do in famous detective stories? Dangerous criminals are known to do that in books!

We had no clue, and so we left.

After coming out of the house, Byomkesh looked at his watch, 'Let's go to the police station. It is not yet ten.'

While going towards the police station, Byomkesh asked, 'You heard the family members; what do you think?'

I was also thinking about it, 'I didn't find any of the family members very upset by the incident.'

Byomkesh said, 'Maybe they are too stunned with grief to react!'

I said, 'But I did not find the behaviour of Ushapati and his wife very normal. It is true that Satyakam was not a good man and they were sick of his behaviour, but even then, he was their son! I feel that there is some great problem in this family.'

'Satyakam himself was a great problem! But what do you think of the tinsel disc on the door?'

'Nothing; did you understand anything?'

'Could be a simple coincidence, but if it is not, then…'

On reaching the police station, we found that we knew the OC. Bhabani babu was an elderly man. He was working at his table and was not pleased to see us. Even so, he showed some politeness and said with an undertone, 'Why are you getting involved in this?'

Byomkesh said, 'I got involved somehow.'

Bhabani babu said with an undertone again, 'The fellow was a rascal. Whoever murdered him has done a good turn to the society, and he should be given a medal.'

Byomkesh said, 'True, you do whatever you think is right. I'll not interfere. I only want to know…'

Bhabani babu gave him a piercing look, 'You want to seek the truth? What do you wish to know?'

'What about the post-mortem report?'

'It will come only in the evening.'

'I will give you a ring later in the evening then.'

'He died of a bullet injury. But it did not pierce him; it is lodged inside his body. The hole on his back is very small. It must have been shot by a pistol or a revolver.'

'That means the person who murdered Satyakam was behind him.'

'Maybe he was hiding in the bushes near the gate. As soon as Satyakam stood in front of the door, he shot him and went out of the gate.'

'There is a bodybuilding school in that area, do you know?'

'I know. It is not their work. They may beat people up but will not murder anyone. They are good, educated boys.'

It was quite surprising to learn that the police thought that educated boys did not commit any crime!

Byomkesh said, 'Talking of educated boys, a cousin of Satyakam stays in the house. Have you seen him?'

Bhabani babu smiled knowingly, 'Yes, I did see him. His name is in the police diary!'

'Really? What did he do?'

'He was a good boy. But in the last riot, his father was killed by Muslim goons. After that, I am sure that he murdered at least three people, but there is no solid proof to arrest him.'

'His eyes are sharp—even I suspect him. Do you think he has something to do with this murder?'

'Maybe. With a rascal like Satyakam around, anything is possible. But he was inside the house when Satyakam was murdered. He and his uncle came out of the house together when they heard Sahadeb scream. Besides, remember, Satyakam was shot from the back.'

Byomkesh asked, 'Was it possible to shoot him from the terrace?'

Bhabani babu said, 'Had the bullet come from the terrace, it would have gone from the body towards the lower part. But the bullet came from the back to the front. So…'

The telephone rang. Bhabani babu spoke on the phone and then said to us, 'I have to leave immediately.'

'We'll also take your leave.' While standing up to leave, Byomkesh asked, 'What were the things Satyakam was carrying when he was murdered?'

'They are in the next room. You can go and see.' Bhabani babu was ready to go.

We went to the next room. There were a few things on the table: the gold cigarette case—which we immediately recognized, a flask of whisky, a leather money bag and a torch. Byomkesh glanced at the articles and we returned to the main office room. Bhabani babu said, 'Have you taken a look? Is there anything more to ask or see? I am leaving now.'

We felt that Bhabani babu would not even try to catch the culprit. Satyakam's murder would remain an unsolved mystery.

We came out of the police station. Byomkesh said, 'Let's go and visit Baag's place, since we have come so far.'

'Will there be anyone there now?'

'Baag could be in his cave!' said Byomkesh jokingly.

But he was not there. A servant informed us that he saw him reading the newspaper in the morning, and immediately after that, he got dressed and said that he was leaving for Benares. The servant was to tell the boys when they came.

We understood that he had read the news and thought it wise to remove himself from the scene.

We returned home at about a quarter past seven. We found Nanda Ghosh walking up and down in front of our door, his face pinched with fear and anxiety. Byomkesh knocked at the door as he asked him, 'What news do you have for us?'

Nanda licked his dry lips, 'Sir…'

Putiram, Byomkesh's Man Friday, opened the door, and we entered the house with Nanda. He hesitated, licked his lips several times and said, 'Have you heard about Satyakam?'

Byomkesh lighted a cigarette and said, 'Yes. Where did you get the news?'

Nanda said, 'I went to the area in the morning to a friend's house and heard that Satyakam was shot dead. I don't know anything, Sir! After you had gone away from the club last evening, I did not go there.'

Byomkesh said, 'I want to ask you a few questions. Do you know of anyone in that area possessing a pistol or a revolver?'

'No Sir, I wouldn't know if anyone had one either.'

'What about someone in your club?'

'I don't know. But a man had once come to sell smuggled pistols to Bhuteshwar Baag.'

'Smuggled pistols?'

'Yes Sir, I heard that they were available in large numbers after the war.'

'Did Baag buy one?'

'Not in front of me.'

'Forget about that. Satyakam was always after girls from respectable houses. How did he win them over?'

Nanda was quiet for sometime, then he said, 'Sir, Satyakam knew magic. He would speak to the girls for a few minutes and put them under his spell. Then he would take them to his shop and give them rich gifts, treated them in restaurants...' Nanda broke off.

'I understand. The girls are also to blame.' Byomkesh took a long drag of his cigarette, paused and said, 'One has to pay a price for the emancipation of women. Anyway, who was he after lately?'

Nanda said uneasily, 'I don't know about everyone, but Akhilesh babu of house number 79 complained in our club that his daughter Shobhona, Ramesar babu's granddaughter, had been trapped by him. There was a big scandal. Anyway, she was married off.'

'Anyone else?'

'And Bhabani babu's daughter, Shalila.'

'Which Bhabani babu?'

'The OC of the neighbouring police station. He locked

up his daughter for sometime and then sent her away to her maternal uncle's house.'

Byomkesh and I glanced at each other. Byomkesh stretched himself and said, 'Okay, Nanda, you may leave for today. Your instructor has fled. You should not go to that area for sometime as well.'

'Okay, Sir,' said Nanda, licking his dry lips.

∽

Byomkesh was distracted the entire day. Satyabati tried to broach the topic of Kashmir in the afternoon, but Byomkesh did not seem to hear anything. He lay on the easy chair and kept staring at the ceiling.

I consoled Satyabati, 'What's the hurry? Let the case be solved.'

Satyabati said, 'It won't take too long to be solved. Can't you see his expression?'

Byomkesh did not hear her but murmured to himself, 'The tinsel disc,' and heaved a deep sigh.

Satyabati gave me a meaningful smile.

We were supposed to call the police station. When I reminded Byomkesh, he said, 'Why don't you call them, Ajit?'

I called the police. Bhabani babu said, 'We received the report just now. The time of death is between midnight and two in the morning. The bullet is from a .45 revolver; the bullet went through the left side, under the scapular, and pierced the heart and then got stuck in the third rib of the right side. The bullet travelled from below to the top, from the side to the centre. There is no sign of any other injury. That's all. Some traces of alcohol were found in the stomach.'

I related this to Byomkesh. Surprised, he stared at me and said, 'What is the path of the bullet, did you say?'

'From below towards the top and from the side to the centre. So whoever fired the shot was hiding in the bushes on the left of the path. He shot the gun while sitting in the bushes.'

Byomkesh stared at me for sometime and said, 'He fired the shot while sitting, why?'

'I don't know. He did not consult me before shooting!'

Byomkesh lay down on the easy chair again and stared at the ceiling, then he slowly said, 'Think about the matter. You think that the criminal had hidden inside the gate. Satyakam walked in through the gate for about twenty to thirty-five feet, stood in front of the main door of the house and knocked at the door, and only then the criminal shot him. I am asking why. He could have shot Satyakam as soon as he came in through the gate. Why did he wait till Satyakam reached the main door? That would have been easier for him; he could have quickly escaped through the gate after shooting Satyakam. There would be no fear of missing his target as well.'

'You tell me what the answer is.'

Byomkesh said, 'The answer is most probably that the murderer did not fire from that side. But I am more worried about the tinsel disc; why did he stick it on the door?'

I asked, 'Oh, that disc is not accidental then?'

'The more I think about it, I believe that it has been put there purposely. It has some deeper significance. If we manage to understand it, the case will be solved.'

I started thinking about the meaning of the tinsel disc. If the murderer had stuck it on the door, then why did he do it? If the murderer did not do it, then who did? If no one in the house had stuck it there, then, was it Satyakam... But why?

Suddenly, Byomkesh sat up and asked, 'Ajit, what are the things that Satyakam carried? What was there on the table at the police station? Do you remember?'

I said, 'There were a few things—a cigarette case, a wrist watch, a money bag, a flask filled with alcohol and an electric torch!'

Byomkesh lay down again, slowly, 'Electric torch? You don't need an electric torch in the streets of Calcutta!'

'No, but you need it to walk from the gate to the main door; it's very dark.'

Byomkesh smiled a little and said, 'Then why didn't Satyakam see his murderer with the torchlight?'

I had no answer to that. After some time, Byomkesh said somewhat disjointedly, 'Tomorrow, we have to speak to Shitangsu alone.'

I looked at him, but he said nothing else and continued with his important task of staring at the ceiling. But I noticed that his expression of dull absentmindedness was replaced by an inner excitement.

∽

Next morning, after getting up, I heard Byomkesh speaking to someone on the phone. I walked to the verandah with a cup of morning tea. Byomkesh too came out soon, his face grim.

I asked, 'Who were you speaking to?'

Byomkesh said, 'Ushapati babu.'

'Why suddenly?'

'I have asked him to send Shitangsu.'

'I see. What's the news in their house?'

'News? The police returned the dead body in the evening. They came back from the crematorium in the early hours today.'

After a pause, Byomkesh said, 'Had the police searched the house yesterday, they would have got the revolver. Now, it won't be there.'

'So the murder was committed by a member of the house?'

Byomkesh did not answer.

Shitangsu came half an hour later.

Byomkesh said, 'Sit down, please. I could not ask you many things yesterday in front of your maternal uncle.'

Shitangsu sat on the chair in front of Byomkesh and stared at him unblinkingly.

Byomkesh started, 'I learnt at the police station yesterday that during the riot, you murdered two or three people. Is that true?'

Shitangsu did not answer but did not look frightened either.

Byomkesh said, 'You may tell me without hesitation, I've nothing to do with the police.'

Shitangsu's throat moved with emotion, 'Yes, they had killed my father.'

Byomkesh lifted his hand, 'I know. What did you use to kill them?'

'A knife.'

'Did you ever use a revolver?'

'No.'

'Did Satyakam have a revolver?'

'I don't know. I don't think so.'

'Is there any revolver in the house?'

'I don't know.'

'Were you friendly with Satyakam?'

'No, we avoided each other.'

'Satyakam was characterless—did you know that?'

'Yes.'

'You loved your father; you must love your sister Chumki a lot too?'

Shitangsu did not answer but stared at Byomkesh. Byomkesh asked all of a sudden, 'Did you ever feel like murdering Satyakam?'

Shitangsu did not answer this question either, but we could

easily interpret his silence.

Byomkesh smiled slightly and said, 'You don't have to say anything, I've understood. You must have threatened Satyakam?'

This time, Shitangsu answered without any hesitation, 'Yes, I told him that if he misbehaved in the house, I'll kill him.'

Byomkesh looked at him for some time—not sharply but a little absentmindedly. Then he said, 'That night, after hearing Sahadeb's shouts, you went to the front door, what did you see there?'

'I saw Satyakam lying face down just outside the main door.'

'How did you see that? Was there a light there?'

'Satyakam was holding a lighted torch, I saw in that light. Then uncle came and switched on the main door light.'

Byomkesh lighted a cigarette. He puffed at it for some time and said, 'Leave all that. There must have been a lot of trouble between your uncle and aunt?'

'Trouble?'

'Yes, quarrelling, scolding...as is usual in such circumstances.'

Shitangsu was quiet for some time and then said, 'No, there was no quarrel, no disturbance.'

'Not at all?'

'No. My uncle and aunt never speak to each other.'

Byomkesh raised his eyebrows in surprise, 'Don't speak to each other? What do you mean?'

'My uncle and aunt never speak to each other.'

'How strange! Since when?'

'Right from the time I have been seeing them. When we stayed in Maniktala, we often used to come to our uncle's house at that time as well. I have never seen them talk.'

'What kind of a person is your aunt—quarrelsome?'

'Not at all. She is a very good person.'

Byomkesh stopped asking questions and shut his eyes as if

in meditation. I remembered last morning, when Ushapati's wife had suddenly entered the room and how Ushapati stared at her with surprise. I could not define his surprise then. Would the divide between the husband and wife close after their son's death?

Byomkesh lay with his eyes closed even after Shitangsu had left. Then he opened his eyes and said with a sigh, 'It's very tragic. How did you find Shitangsu?'

'I felt that he was telling the truth.'

Byomkesh said, 'The boy is clever, very clever,' and again closed his eyes. Half an hour later, he woke up from his meditation to the sound of the doorbell. I got up to open the door to Ushapati.

Byomkesh welcomed Ushapati and offered him a seat. Ushapati looked extremely tired even as he sat on a chair. His eyes were slightly red and his body seemed to be breaking down with exhaustion. Byomkesh gave him a cigarette. Both stared at each other questioningly. Ushapati said, 'I went to the police station after receiving your call. But they don't seem to know anything. So I came to you for some news.'

Ushapati's words seemed to hold a question that Byomkesh did not tackle directly. He simply said, 'It is not a one-day affair, Ushapati babu; it will take time. You look completely exhausted; you should not have come out of your house today. Besides, your wife too needs looking after.'

I was watching Ushapati's expression; his face did not register any change at the mention of his wife. There was no indication there of the estrangement between the two of them for years.

He just said, 'I am worried about her. She is devastated.' He added after a while, 'I am thinking that I'll take her on a trip somewhere. If we go out of Calcutta, she will feel better, in my mind.'

'True, where will you go? Have you decided on a place?'

'No, anywhere outside Calcutta. But won't the police object?'

'Inform the police before you go. I don't think they will object.'

'If they don't object, then we'll leave tomorrow or the day after. Calcutta is like poison to me. All right, I'll leave now.' Ushapati stood up to leave.

Byomkesh asked, 'Will your shop remain closed?'

'Suchitra Emporium? No, no. There's Dhananjoy babu, a very old employee, the cashier, a very trusted person; he will look after the Emporium. I am thinking of asking my nephew Shitu, as well, to look after the business. After all, we have nobody else.'

'Are you going to your shop now?'

'No I won't go to the shop. I'll call Dhananjoy babu and let him know.'

'All right then, goodbye.'

Byomkesh finished three cigarettes at a stretch after Ushapati left. Then he stood up and said, 'I am going out, you stay at home.'

'Where are you going?'

'To Suchitra Emporium—to meet the cashier, Dhananjoy babu. I need to have a talk with him.'

It was past one-thirty in the afternoon when Byomkesh returned. I was waiting after having my bath; Satyabati was pacing restlessly in and out of the room.

Byomkesh entered, opened his shirt, switched on the fan and laid flat on the bed. It was pretty hot, although it was spring in Calcutta.

I said, 'You seem to have quite enjoyed your chat with the cashier.'

Byomkesh said, 'Do you know who that person was? The

cashier who had given us the cash memo the day before yesterday.'

'Really? So what did you get from him?'

'Yes, I got something,' he looked up at the revolving fan and smiled, 'A loving gift!'

'A loving gift!'

'Yes, about twenty or twenty-five years back, it was a very popular practice to print this loving gift in the form of a poem on fine paper, in red ink, on the occasion of a wedding. You must have seen it.'

'Yes, the cashier gave you that?'

'It is in the upper pocket of my shirt, take it out.'

'But it's for whose wedding?'

'Why don't you read it?'

I took the paper out of his pocket. It was a thin paper with writing in red ink and a flying butterfly placed on top. Encircling the butterfly were the words, 'The Wedding of Suchitra and Ushapati'. Then came the poem. I don't believe that there is any wise man under the sun who would be able to decipher the meaning of the poem. At the end was the name of the poet: Dhananjoy Mondal and the workers of Suchitra Emporium.

I said, 'There might be some historical value of this poem; did you get nothing except this?'

'I don't need anything else—everything is in this paper. Oh my blind friend! Check properly!'

I read the poem again, even though I found it very difficult to read it. Then I said, 'If there is any hidden meaning in the poem, then I am sorry I cannot understand it. Suchitra must be the name of Ushapati's wife. The workers of Suchitra Emporium and Dhananjoy Mondal were delighted at the marriage of the two—this is all I can understand.'

'Not the poem, my dear Watson, the date…the date of the wedding!'

The date was written on the lower-left side of the paper: Calcutta, 13 February 1927.

I said, 'I saw the date, but I am still in the dark.'

'Byomkesh sat up,' Remember Satyakam telling us his birthday and year?'

'Yes, but I don't remember the date.'

'I remember.'

I said impatiently, 'What is the meaning behind the dates? What is the connection between these dates and Satyakam's death?'

'A very crucial connection, I believe.'

'If you have understood who has committed the crime, tell me frankly.'

'You can't understand?'

'No... Who killed Satyakam?'

'Ushapati babu!'

'The father has killed the son?'

'It would be okay if he did. But Satyakam is not his son.'

I was totally puzzled and sat like a zombie.

Satyabati peeped in and said sarcastically, 'Are you going to fast today?'

ᴄ⁀ɔ

Around four in the afternoon, Ushapati came again. This time too, he came unannounced. But this time, he was not looking tired or sad, as in the morning. His expression was sharp and alert. He sat in front of Byomkesh, stared at him sharply and said, 'You went to meet Dhananjoy babu?'

Byomkesh said quietly, 'Yes, I did.'

'What was your query?'

'Whatever I wanted to know, I did.'

'What did you get to know?'

'Everything, Ushapati babu. Even the mystery behind the tinsel disc on the front door of your house.'

The sharp questions of Ushapati were blunted by this answer. He stared again at Byomkesh for some time and then said in a controlled voice, 'Will you be able to prove all of it in a court of law?'

Byomkesh said, 'Your wedding date and Satyakam's date of birth, perhaps; but about the other things, I doubt it. But Ushapati babu, I don't want to prove anything, I only wish to know. Satyakam had asked me to find his murderer. He did not ask me to hand him over to the police. That is not my responsibility.'

Ushapati stared at Byomkesh with unblinking eyes. Slowly, his expression changed. A minute ago, he was ready to battle it out with Byomkesh, and now his aggressive stance was totally gone. He said in an incredulous voice, 'You won't tell the police what you have found?'

Byomkesh said, 'No! Why should I? The police do not want my help!'

Ushapati took out a handkerchief from his pocket and covered his face with it. His body trembled a few times with emotion. When he looked up again, we saw that his expression had changed completely. It was the expression of a terminal patient who had just recovered from his illness. He sat quietly for some time and then said in a broken voice, 'Byomkesh babu, do you want to know why Satyakam had to die?'

Byomkesh said, 'Yes, you must tell me everything.'

Ushapati looked at me hesitantly and it was very clear that though he was ready to reveal all to Byomkesh, he was unwilling to do so in the presence of another.

Byomkesh understood him, 'Ajit, why don't you go to Howrah station and find out about the trains going to Kashmir from the enquiry, whether there is still trouble going on there and so on? It is better to get all the information beforehand.'

I was disappointed. I changed and went out.

∽

It was evening when I returned from Howrah station. Ushapati had left by that time. In the semi-darkness of the room, Byomkesh and Satyabati were sitting intimately. The southern wind was pleasantly blowing in through the open window. Satyabati moved away when she saw me entering.

I came in and said, 'You were enjoying the southern breeze like two lovebirds. Where is Khoka?'

Satyabati said shyly, 'Putiram has taken him to the park to play.'

Byomkesh said, 'The poets are not liars. Everyone becomes restless with the onset of spring and there is ample reason for that. It does not affect only the youth but also the not so young. I believe that if it was not springtime, then Ushapati would not have killed Satyakam.'

I said sarcastically, 'What are you saying? The poets have never ever romanticized about such a terrible influence of spring!'

Byomkesh said, 'Yes, yes! They have written about it in innuendoes and not in a straightforward manner. *Fire gives light, but it burns too.* Anyway, what about Kashmir?'

I said, 'There is a war going on in Kashmir and ordinary people are not allowed to enter. If you wish to go, you will need a permit from the Government of India.'

I pulled a chair and sat next to Byomkesh.

He said, 'It will not be difficult to get a permit. I am at present on very good terms with the government, at least till Vallabhbhai Patel is alive. But the thing is, should we all go to Kashmir? Khoka has just started going to school and his summer vacation is nowehere near. He should not miss school, I feel.'

Satyabati said, 'But why should Khoka go? He will stay at home. Ajit dada, won't you be able to look after Khoka?'

I stared at Satyabati for some time and said, 'So this is your plot! The two of you will fly to Kashmir like two swans, and I'll stay with Khoka at home! Byomkesh, you are right; spring is indeed a dangerous season. But it's fine with me. You two can go and I'll happily stay here with Khoka. To tell you the truth, I had no desire to go to Kashmir. I feel Calcutta is the best place in the whole world!'

I took a cigarette from Byomkesh's packet. Satyabati hid a smile. Byomkesh recited a poem,

Youth is the sweetest time
before time destroys it.
Enjoy, therefore, as much as you can.

Byomkesh then asked for a cigarette and I handed him one. I said to him, 'You have ruined your character by reading too many poems. But tell us, do you mind relating the "homily" that Ushapati had recited to you?'

'Not at all. I was, in fact, waiting for you to come back. I'll tell you both. It's a very sad tale.'

Byomkesh began, 'Satyakam had come to me with a strange proposal, "If I die suddenly, you will investigate my death." He already knew who wanted to kill him but did not tell me his name. I have wondered, why did he not reveal the name of the person he suspected would kill him? Now I know why he didn't. He had all the reason not to tell me, or else the family scandal would be out in the open. That he was an illegitimate child and that his mother had a dark past was difficult for him to tell me. Anyway, how many people can reveal such a disgusting truth? Not everyone can be the Satyakam of the scriptures.

'He had given me a hint; nevertheless, he told us his date of birth. But he did it in such a way that no one would suspect that the key to the mystery of his death was concealed in that little detail! He knew that if I started investigating, his birth date would be useful to me. Satyakam was an immoral lecher, but he was extremely intelligent.

'Now I'll tell you the story from the beginning. It starts from before Satyakam's birth. It is Ushapati who told me most of the story, yet I am sure that the story is true. He did not spare himself; he did not hide his faults and weaknesses. He revealed everything.

'In the first half of the twentieth century, Ramakanto Choudhury established Suchitra Emporium. His only child was his daughter, Suchitra, and the emporium was named after her. He was a clever businessman, and so within two years, his business began to flourish. He constructed a new building in Dharamtala. His emporium was competing with the existing English stores of the time.

'Ushapati took a job as a small shop assistant in Suchitra Emporium in the year 1925. He was only twenty-one or twenty-two. He was an orphan from a good family but did not have much education. He was good-looking and intelligent. In a few days, he learnt the art of handling customers and making them happy. He was very popular among his colleagues. Soon, the owner himself noticed him, and he began earning increments.

'Two years went by. Then Ushapati's luck smiled on him all of a sudden. Ramakanto Choudhury called him to his chamber and said, "I want to give my daughter's hand in marriage to you." This proposal was beyond Ushapati's imagination. It was like the fairy tale in which the princess was married to a beggar. Ushapati had seen Suchitra several times in the Emporium, she looked sweet and soft. Ushapati's heart overflowed with romance!

'They were married within a month. It was a grand wedding. Ushapati's colleagues gave him the loving gift of a poem and congratulated him. All this while, Ushapati had stayed in the house of his married sister, and now he shifted to the house of his father-in-law at Amherst Street. Ramakanto was a widower and did not want to part with his daughter after her marriage.

'Ushapati found out on the night of his wedding that the golden wrapper of the gift had a knife hidden inside. His dreams crumbled around him. He realized why the affluent owner of Suchitra Emporium had arranged the wedding of his only daughter with a poor man like him. He did not sleep in the luxurious bed covered with flowers. He spent the night sitting on a chair. The very next morning, he went to his father-in-law and told him that now since the gentleman's plan had been executed, his pawn would like to leave.

'Ramakanto was a seasoned businessman and he was probably expecting such a reaction. He explained to his new son-in-law that Suchitra was a young, motherless girl, without anyone to guide her. Besides, with such a modern lifestyle, the young girl lost control over herself. Suchitra was a good girl and only because of her present circumstance, she had made a mistake. It was happening in nearly all affluent households, he explained to Ushapati, and no one gets to know. Everyone lived happily ever after. If Ushapati made any noise about it, he will be a part of the whole scandal.

'But Ushapati was not to be convinced with those words, and he said, "I am poor, but I belong to a good family, I cannot carry on with this."

'When Ramakanto found that it was not easy to convince the young man, he played his trump card. He took out a document from his almirah and said, "From today, you are an equal partner in Suchitra Emporium. You have a fifty per cent partnership. Look at this document—when I die, the two of you will get everything I possess; I have no one else. But from today onwards, you are my partner. Everyone in the shop will look up to you and obey you as they do with me."

'Ushapati was stunned by this offer. It was true that the princess came with a sordid history, but he was also getting half of the kingdom that was without any stain whatsoever. How could he refuse? He agreed, because he could not resist the temptation of possessing so much of wealth. He agreed to stay on in the house of his father-in-law. But there was no relationship between the husband and wife. They did not even talk to each other and began sleeping in separate rooms. The outsiders, of course, were no wiser.

'But what Ramakanto had said about his daughter was, indeed, true. Suchitra was a good girl. The wind of excessive freedom and free-mixing, together with the absence of motherly guidance, had taken Suchitra out of her ken, and without realizing it, she had fallen into a vortex of sensual temptations. When reality struck her like a thunderbolt, she confined herself to the house. She would not go out at all. There were only three people in the house—Ramakanto, Suchitra and Ushapati, besides the very old servant, Sahadeb. The others came and went. Sahadeb was a simpleton and very loyal. So no word went out of the house.

'After a month and a half of the wedding, Ramakanto went abroad with his daughter. He told the outside world that his daughter was unwell, and he was taking her out for treatment. Ushapati became the virtual master of the emporium.

'He returned after nearly a year, with his daughter and her little son. No one could make out whether the child was two months or five months old.

'Then began Ushapati's barren, lifeless existence at Amherst Street. He had no intimacy with his wife and only a working relationship with his father-in-law. He loved the shop as his own, but even so, an enormous emptiness often devoured his young heart. In the meantime, Suchitra confined herself in her room and became a recluse. Ushapati did see her sometimes, she looked like a strict ascetic. He felt a softness towards her, but he forced himself to be strong and stay away from her.

'Years went by. Satyakam began growing up. The bloodline of an indisciplined, debauched father began to present itself in him. He was beyond anyone's control. He did whatever he wanted to, but he was very cunning and intelligent. His grandfather was so enamoured with him that he could not say anything to the boy. Suchitra tried to control him but failed.

'Ushapati avoided any contact with Satyakam—what man has any love for his illegitimate son? Had Satyakam been a good boy, Ushapati would perhaps have tolerated him, but now his mind was poisoned against Satyakam. There could have been a working relationship between Ushapati and Suchitra, but Satyakam was like a poison creeper—a barbed wire between the two.

'When Satyakam was nineteen years of age, his grandfather, Ramakanto, died, leaving his share to his grandson in his will. It was during this time that Satyakam got to know about the secret of his birth. He was born in England, and there was a birth certificate. He had probably got that certificate from among the papers of his grandfather. Things became crystal clear to him. Outwardly, Satyakam was very suave and smart, but he was by nature extremely jealous and cunning. His behaviour with Suchitra and Ushapati became progressively vicious. One day, he told Suchitra to her face, "How dare you try to meddle with me? I know everything!" He told Ushapati, "Why should I bother about paying you any respect? Are you my father?"

'The life of the "seeming" couple became quite unbearable. In the meantime, Satyakam showed another aspect of his character in the shop. He began to impose his "right" as an equal partner. The emporium was an expensive and luxurious shopping experience. Its customers were mostly rich women, rather than males. Satyakam now began to choose young, pretty female customers and became over-friendly with them. He would give them expensive gifts from the shop, take them to fancy restaurants and win them over. For all these exploits, he would take large amounts of money from the cash box of the shop. Gambling, drinking, frequenting the race courses and visiting posh clubs of the city became an everyday affair for him.

'Within a year of Ramakanto's death, the financial graph of the shop began to decline precariously. Whenever Ushapati tried to stop Satyakam, he was told, "I am spending my own money; what's it to you?"

'Over and above all this, the shop began to gather a bad reputation. People began to say that it was not safe for young women to go to the shop. The number of buyers began to dwindle. Ushapati was driven to distraction with worry. He did not know what to do.

'An incident that occurred at that time added fuel to the fire. One evening, Ushapati had come back to the house. As he was about to enter his room, he heard a muffled sobbing sound coming from the next room, which was Suchitra's bedroom. Quietly, he went to the door and found that his wife was hitting her head on the floor and crying bitterly, "Is my penance not over as yet? I am unable to bear any more."

'Ushapati came downstairs as quietly as he could. He asked the old servant Sahadeb what had happened. He came to know that an elderly woman from the neighbourhood had come to meet Suchitra and had insulted her with harsh words. Satyakam was taking the daughter of that lady out every day to watch films and to eat at restaurants.

'Ushapati came to a decision that very moment. Satyakam had to go. It was no use living under this terrible curse called Satyakam.

'Ushapati started making preparations. He had an advantage. No one would suspect him if Satyakam was murdered, because to the outside world, he was Satyakam's father. It was unheard of that a father would kill his only son. Moreover, Satyakam had a lot of enemies because of his wayward ways. The suspicion, naturally, would fall on them. Still, he would have to be careful so that no one should suspect him in any way. Ushapati made a foolproof plan. He bought a revolver from a clandestine source. In his youth, he had been drawn to the revolutionaries, so he knew how to use firearms. He went and practised shooting in a lonely garden plot for a few days. Then he waited for his opportunity.

'Satyakam had the mind of a criminal. He somehow suspected Ushapati and gauged his intention. But he could not find any means to save himself. Had he gone to the police, his date of birth would be exposed. At last, he came to me. Ushapati, of course, knew nothing about this.

'It was on a Saturday night that Satyakam was murdered. On this day of the week, Satyakam came home later than usual. So, Ushapati decided that Saturday had to be the day. He made a tinsel disc. At ten-thirty at night, when Sahadeb went to the kitchen, Ushapati came down quietly and stuck the shining tinsel disc on the outside of the main door, a little lower, near the door knob. No one got to know about it. Then Sahadeb finished his dinner, locked the front door and lay down just inside the door, ready to open it when Satyakam would knock late at night. On the floor above, Ushapati waited in a dark room with the balcony door open.

'After waiting for hours, he heard a noise at the gate...

Satyakam was coming! Ushapati came out on the balcony and waited for him in the dark. The path from the gate to the main door was dark. With a lighted torch in hand, Satyakam was coming towards the main door of the house. He knocked at the door once; then, in the light of the torch, the shining tinsel disc caught his eye. He leaned a little to see what it was. Ushapati, who had been waiting precisely for that moment, shot at him from the balcony. The bullet pierced Satyakam's back and got stuck in his ribs. It looked as if he had been shot from the back. Satyakam fell on his face. The torch continued to be lit.

'This is the real story behind Satyakam's death. Ushapati had done the deed so cleverly that it seemed that Satyakam was shot from the back. It was impossible to make out that someone had shot at him from the top. If it were not for the tinsel disc, even I would not have understood.'

Byomkesh stopped speaking. We, too, were quiet for quite some time. Satyabati heaved a sigh and asked, 'When did you first suspect Ushapati?'

Byomkesh said, 'I had a hunch right at the beginning that it was the work of some family member—an insider's job. I felt that there must have been some family scandal. Had the threat really come from outside, Satyakam would have surely told me who he suspected was behind this planned murder.

'Then I got to know that the married life of Ushapati and Suchitra was not a normal one at all. Their rooms were separate, and they did not speak to each other. I became doubtful about a few things.

'I met the cashier and chatted him up. He really had great affection for Ushapati. It was he who had written the poem that was gifted to the couple during the wedding. Dhananjoy babu had kept it with great care because that was the first and last of his literary achievements! I got the wedding invitation, along with the poem. All my doubts were set to rest once I read it. I remembered that Satyakam had especially mentioned his date of birth on the day he came to meet me—14 July 1927. The wedding date of Suchitra and Ushapati was 13 February 1927. That is, Satyakam was born five months after the wedding. There was no doubt why the cunning Ramakanto had given his daughter's hand to a poor worker in the emporium.

'Satyakam was not Ushapati's son, so Ushapati had no affection for him. Besides, Satyakam was indeed the proverbial black sheep. He put the rest of the family in constant worry. There was every possibility that Ushapati would kill him. But how did he kill Satyakam? When I heard that Satyakam always carried a torch and that the lighted torch was found beside his dead body, I became sure about the role of the tinsel disc. When Satyakam saw the disc in the light of his torch, he bent down out of curiosity to see what it really was, and Ushapati used the opportunity to the hilt.'

Everyone was quiet for some time. I handed Byomkesh a cigarette, and the two of us smoked in silence for a while. The room was dark, the southern wind was blowing around us.

Byomkesh said suddenly, 'Before leaving, Ushapati told me today, "My wife and I have suffered immensely in life for the last twenty-one years. We want to forget the past and live a new life. We want to be happy again. Please let us live." He had held my hand. I have given my word to Ushapati. I know what I am doing is not strictly legal but some things are above legality. Do you think I have done something wrong?'

Satyabati and I replied in unison, 'No! No!'

7

The One and Only
Adwitiya

I, Ajit, always enjoyed myself immensely whenever Satyabati and Byomkesh had a fierce marital quarrel—though I never took sides and was always impartial. But whenever the argument hovered on the comparative qualities of males and females, I was duty-bound, as a male, to support Byomkesh. But I must admit that both of us together were no match for Satyabati. The problem was that the vices of men had been listed in history in such great numbers that it was impossible to dispute. So at the end of the day, we have to admit defeat.

Calcutta was beset with a new problem for the last few days. Byomkesh and I were discussing this one winter morning over a cup of tea. The problem was more or less like this: During mid afternoons, when housewives were ready to take a nap after lunch in the absence of their office-going husbands, a group of young ladies, presumably from a decent background, knocked at their doors. If any housewife was alert, she would ask who it was without opening the door. The group of young ladies would say that they had beautifully embroidered things for ladies at a very nominal price. Curiosity overcame caution and the door would open to allow the erstwhile saleswoman or women in. On entering, the house would be looted of cash and ornaments at gunpoint.

These incidents were becoming quite frequent, but the criminals were still roaming free.

I opened the newspaper and found that a similar incident had occurred in Kasipore. I read out the news item for Byomkesh. He gave a crooked smile and said, 'Why are you surprised? It is a habit of women to plunder during the afternoon in the absence of their husbands.'

Satyabati entered with a frown and said, 'Women plunder, and men are all saints!'

Byomkesh was caught unawares but was not ready to backtrack, 'I am not saying that all men are saints, but neither are women.'

A heated argument ensued. Satyabati sat on one corner of the divan and said, 'You have a habit of speaking ill of women—what have we done?'

Byomkesh said sarcastically, 'Nothing much, they loot houses during lonely afternoon hours!'

I read out the news item, this time to Satyabati.

Satyabati said, 'They are doing it because of poverty, but men commit murders and start wars that kill thousands. What do you have to say about that? How many murders have women committed?'

Her argument was solid.

Byomkesh said fumblingly, 'All these years, women were homebound, so they did not get a chance. Now with women's emancipation, no one can guess where all this will end. Bankim Chandra had written about the great bandit queen, Debi Choudhurani, years ago. If she were here now, can you imagine what would be the shape of things?'

Satyabati said, 'Don't beat around the bush. Give me true incidents in which women have actually murdered people.'

Byomkesh said, 'You want incidents? Only the other day—

maybe two months back—a female criminal murdered a jail guard and escaped.'

Satyabati laughed, 'Two months ago, a female criminal killed one guard; how many murders have males committed within these two months?'

There was an incident of a murder in the paper that day, but I kept quiet about it. Instead, to make light of things, I said, 'I read about the cruelty of a woman in today's paper: A washerman had spoiled her favourite expensive saree, so she lost her temper and cut his nose with a sharp knife. The poor washerman is in the hospital in a critical condition!'

Satyabati said, 'You are liars as well—along with being thieves, robbers and murderers!'

We were all warming up to a heated argument when there was a knock at the door. Triumphant, Satyabati departed. I opened the door and found the postman waiting outside. He delivered a thick envelope and left.

It was addressed to Byomkesh; there was no sender's name. Byomkesh pressed the envelope with his fingers and said, 'It must be a manuscript sent by a fledgling writer; send it to Prabhat.'

After we got involved in the publication business, we had been flooded with manuscripts from enthusiastic writers. Byomkesh was a little apprehensive about this.

I reassured him, 'It may not be a manuscript. Why don't you open it?'

He said, 'You open it.'

I opened the envelope. It was not a manuscript but a rather long letter addressed to Byomkesh and was the size of a short story. Byomkesh was somewhat relieved, 'It's not a love letter, so you can read it, and I'll listen.'

So, he lay down on the divan. I pulled up a chair near him and started reading. The handwriting was not clear, it took some effort to read it. But the style and flow were easy.

Respected Byomkesh babu,

My name is Chintamoni Kundu. The police are trying to entrap me in a murder case. I am helpless and request for protection and help from you. If I had the strength, I would have met you personally. If I could present my case face to face, it would have been more effective, but for the last few years, I have been debilitated by paralysis. I can move a few steps in my room only. So I have been forced to write this letter to you.

Before I describe the terrible thing that has happened here, I would like to tell you a few things about myself. I am fifty-seven years old; I have no wife or children. I have only three houses. I have let out the houses, and in one of these three houses on rent, I occupy two rooms on the second floor. My servant, Ramadhin, looks after my needs.

You will understand, after seeing my address in this letter, that I live in the south-eastern part of Calcutta. The street in front of my house is quite broad, and the house in which I live is on one side of the road. My other two houses are on the opposite side of the road, quite nearby and visible from the house where I stay. Those two houses are relatively small and one-storeyed; one can call them twin houses. There is a small alley between the two houses that leads to their back doors.

Since I am paralytic, my life is limited to my two rooms. Before my condition became like this, I was an agent and had to run around a lot. I was used to a busy life. Now I sit next to my window and watch the comings and goings of people on the street below. I have bought a pair of binoculars with which I see distant things at a close range. I can keep a watch over my twin houses and can sometimes even see what is happening inside them. Able-bodied people go to cinemas, I sit next to my window and watch the flow of life and, with the binoculars, even watch what is happening behind the scenes. But let me come to the main issue.

About a month and a half back, in the middle of January, a young man had come to meet me. He was short, had brownish hair, an intelligent expression and adorned a butterfly moustache. He wore an expensive western suit and over it, a camel hair overcoat. He stood outside my door and said respectfully, 'My name is Tapan Sen, may I come inside?'

I was sitting next to my window and reading a newspaper. I said, 'Come in.'

Tapan Sen pulled up a chair and sat in front of me. I asked, 'What do you want?'

He pointed outside the window and said, 'One of your twin houses is vacant, so I have come to request you to let it out to me.'

The house had been vacant for some time. The previous tenant had left it in a bad state. I had got it repaired and whitewashed. I had decided that I would not rent it out if I did not get a good tenant. I felt that this young man was quite good. By the way he was dressed, he looked quite well-to-do as well. I asked him, 'What do you do?'

He pulled out a cigarette case from his overcoat pocket, then kept it back again, probably as a sign of respect for an elderly person like me. He said, 'I work in a newspaper agency as an editor. I work the whole night through and sleep the whole day,' he smiled.

I asked, 'What about your family?'

He said with a smile, 'I have just started a family—my wife and myself; there is no one else.'

I was quite pleased. Children often destroy houses and

disfigure walls. I said, 'All right, I'll give the house to you. The rent is one hundred and fifty rupees.'

He hesitated a little, 'It is a little too high for me.'

I said, 'It is a furnished house, you will get a bedstead, cupboard, tables, chairs—everything.'

He said, 'All right, I'll take it. Can I see the house?'

I gave him the keys. He went and saw the house. Then he took out a hundred and fifty rupees and said, 'Take this rent money for a month.'

I gave him a receipt and said, 'When will you occupy the house?'

He said, 'Tomorrow is the first of the month. If you permit, then I'll come today itself.'

I said, 'I have no problem. You may come anytime you wish.'

Tapan went off with the keys. I was happy to think that I had got a good tenant.

The whole day, I sat by the window and watched. But Tapan did not arrive with his wife. The next morning, I opened the window and found that they had already come. The front door was open. They must have moved in some time in the previous evening.

My curious eyes kept going back to the house. Around half past nine, a young woman came and shut the front door from inside and after a few minutes, came out of the back door, through the alley.

I saw her then—she was slim and tall and had an abundant head of hair, which she had collected in a bun at the nape of her neck. I thought, Tapan must be sleeping after his work at night, so his wife was going to the market.

But morning turned to noon, still the woman did not return. She returned at about four in the afternoon. She did not knock on the front door but walked through the alley to the back door. She probably did not want to disturb her sleeping husband.

After some time, I sent Ramadhin. They had just arrived, so I felt it was my duty to find out if they needed anything. I saw from my window that Ramadhin was knocking at the door. It was opened by the young woman. After speaking to Ramadhin, she looked up at my window and then with Ramadhin, she came up to my floor.

I had seen her from a distance and now I saw her in person. She was a good-looking, tall and slim young woman. She had a small, reddish mole on her left cheek that made her look more attractive. I noticed that the husband and wife were of the same age—about twenty-three or twenty-four. They must have fallen in love and married, I thought.

She greeted me and said, 'My name is Shanta. We have no problem. We have got a beautiful house.' She had an endearing way of speaking. Her voice was sweet and melodious as well.

I said, 'Please sit.'

She said, 'Please don't speak so formally with me. I am like your daughter.'

I said, 'If you want any daily worker to do your chores, let me know; you have come to a new area.'

She said, 'We don't need any domestic help. We are just two of us, so I can manage the household chores.'

I said, 'You went out in the morning and have just returned. Where did you go?'

She said, 'I teach in a school. There is a small girls' school near Chetla—I teach there. Let me go now. I have to cook food for my husband. He will go out in the evening.' Shanta smiled and left.

I liked the young couple. Right now, I have no one else

in my life except the tenants. The others live in my house, pay rent and are busy with their own lives. They have no time for me.

A South Indian couple lives in the other part of the twin house. We cannot understand each other's language; they just pay the rent at the end of the month, take the receipt and leave. I have no affection for them. But I began to have a soft corner for this young, newlywed Bengali couple.

From my window, I noticed that after dark, Tapan, in his coat, pants and overcoat left through the back door, stopped under the lamp post to light a cigarette, and turned towards the main road. I understood that he would work through the night and return home early next morning.

From then on, this same routine continued. Around nine-thirty in the morning, Shanta went out to teach and came back in the afternoon. Tapan went out in the evening, and at what time he returned, I did not know. No one came to their house, perhaps they had no friends or relatives nearby.

After Tapan left in the evening, the electric light inside the house would be switched off, only a mild candle light could be seen in the room at the front. That too went off at about eight in the evening. Shanta probably retires to bed early after a day's hard work.

I was quite curious about the couple. So, I often watched them through my binoculars. But I could not see anything inside the house. The front door was always shut, and the curtains of the windows were always drawn. Only at night, the dim light of the candle could be seen through the curtains.

One Sunday morning, Shanta came to my house and spent some time with me. I asked jokingly, 'So is your dear husband still sleeping?'

She said shyly, 'Yes, he cannot sleep at all at night.'

I said, 'You do not switch on the electric light at night, I have noticed, why?'

Shanta looked somewhat startled, then she said, 'My eyes are bad, I cannot bear the strain of bright lights. But my husband cannot see in dim light. So, as soon as he leaves, I stop using the electric light and light a lamp or a candle. You have noticed that?'

'Yes, I sit at the window from morning till evening.'

Shanta said sympathetically, 'Really, you have nowhere to go? I'll come whenever I have time, I'll ask my husband to come too.'

Days were passing by. One evening, Tapan also came and chatted with me before going for work.

Then I noticed something in the middle of one night.

I usually retire to bed by nine-thirty every night. But I suffer from insomnia and sometimes stay awake the whole night. About two weeks back, I went to bed at my usual time but could not sleep at all… I tried to sleep till midnight, then got up from bed. I thought that if I had a cup of warm cocoa, I might be able to sleep. So I put some water on a stove. Ramadhin sleeps just outside my door but I did not want to disturb him.

It was a winter night, and so the window was closed. I do not know what came over me all of a sudden, but I opened the window a little and looked outside. It was the dead of the night. There was not a soul in sight. Only a lone streetlight was shining in front of the twin houses. The inside of both the houses were dark.

I saw a person walking on the opposite footpath. He was wrapped in a black shawl. Coming right in front of the two houses, he looked around and slipped quickly into the narrow alley between the twin houses. I could not see him again, but after some time, the electric light in Tapan's house was switched on and then quickly switched off again!

As I sipped on my cocoa, I began wondering who that strange midnight visitor could be. He seemed surreptitiously careful. One can access the South Indian tenant's back door through that alley as well, but they lock all their doors and turn in by evening. So that person definitely went in through the back door of Tapan's house. Tapan was not at home at that time and Shanta was all alone. What was going on? In the dead of the night, with the husband being absent and only a young woman there in the house.... What was that man doing there? He was wrapped in a shawl too, so that no one could see his face! All that pointed to only one thing... Oh! It was so obvious!

I felt disappointed and depressed. I had thought that Shanta was a good girl, but it was indeed difficult to assess a woman's character. But whatever it was, why should I be bothered about what my tenant's wife was doing? It was enough if I got my rent regularly.

I thought for a moment that I would watch from my window to see when the man would come out of the house. But after the cup of hot cocoa, I felt a little drowsy and did not want to spoil my night's sleep.

Two weeks went by after that. Last Sunday, Tapan came and gave me the house rent. Nothing striking had happened in the meantime. I did not mention to Tapan anything about the nocturnal guest of his wife. After all, it was none of my business.

Then, an incident occurred the night before last. That night too, I had difficulty sleeping. I tossed in bed till midnight. Then I got up and put some water on the stove for my cup of *cocoa. I opened my window out of curiosity. It was as if the man from that earlier night was waiting for me to open the window and peer through it. He quickly walked to the alley and hid a little inside. Then I saw another man coming down the same footpath. This man had a muffler around his neck. He walked up to the alley and looked around uncertainly. It seemed to me that he was following the first shawl-wrapped man, and now he was unable to trace him.*

The shawl-wrapped man was obviously lying in wait for his follower. Now he removed the shawl from his face and to my surprise, I saw that it was none other than Tapan! A terrible thing happened within a second or two. With a sharp knife flashing in his hand, Tapan jumped in front of the muffler-wearing fellow and drove the knife right into his chest! The man fell on the footpath. Tapan disappeared into the alley in a flash.

The sudden and unexpected incident left me petrified and stunned. The man lay on the footpath without even uttering a cry. He must have died instantaneously.

I have a telephone in my room. After recovering a little, I called up the police station, which is near my house. The police arrived within five minutes. After hearing about the whole incident from me, the officer-in-charge surrounded Tapan's house.

But Tapan was not found in the house. Shanta was sleeping, and she knew nothing about what had happened. It was certain that Tapan had entered the house through the back door. He must have changed his clothes and escaped quietly, without Shanta being aware of anything.

The dead body could not be identified that night. Later, it was found that the deceased was one Bidhubhushan Aich, an officer of the Burdwan Police Station, who was on leave and had come to Calcutta recently.

The police are posted at Tapan's house presently. Tapan is still absconding. The officers have made poor Shanta's life hell by constantly interrogating her. But she is innocent. I had suspected her earlier unnecessarily. Now I realize that it was Tapan who wrapped himself in a shawl and came home at midnight.

The police have made my condition unbearable too. I have no idea why Tapan had killed the man, but every now and then, new officers from the police department keep harassing me. I am a paralysed, handicapped person, but I feel that the police are suspicious of me. My only fault is that Tapan is my tenant, and I had witnessed the crime.

I am ardently begging you to save me from this situation. I am unable to bear it any longer. I fear that the police would arrest me and put me in jail for no fault of mine. I'll surely die then. I have money. If you can save me from this predicament, I assure you that I'll make you happy. Please rescue me from the police. I'll be forever grateful to you.

Yours entreatingly,
Chintamoni Kundu

After I had finished reading the letter, Byomkesh took it from me and began reading it silently. I moved towards the kitchen in hopes for a cup of tea and also to pacify Satyabati who had walked off in a huff.

Coming back after about half an hour, I found Byomkesh sitting with the letter on his lap and smiling to himself. I asked, 'What's so amusing?'

Byomkesh said, 'The whole thing is amusing. Chintamoni Kundu, however, has made a mistake about one thing—the time of the electric light being switched off in Tapan's house.'

'How did you know that?'

'If my guess is right, he has made a mistake. He has made another mistake, but that is understandable.'

Byomkesh began smiling meaningfully again. Then composing his face, he said, 'Ajit, Chintamoni babu has a phone in his room, find out the number and call him up. I need an answer to an important question. Please ask him what is the sound of Tapan's voice.'

I said sarcastically, 'Indeed an important question, anything else you wish to know?'

'No, nothing else. Tell him not to worry, I'll visit him soon.'

I called up Chintamoni, then came back to inform Byomkesh, 'Tapan's voice is hoarse.'

Byomkesh said, 'Hoarse! Then I was right—there is no doubt now.'

I said, 'God knows what you have understood, but Chintamoni's voice is hoarse as well!'

Byomkesh said, 'That could be too with so many years of being paralysed and on top of that, being harassed by the police. Let's go, we'll have lunch after we return.'

∽

The street to Chintamoni's house was quite wide and new. As it was on the outskirts of the city, it was comparatively quiet. We could easily identify Tapan's house by seeing the police milling about. Chintamoni's house was on the opposite side of the street. It was a double-storeyed house. We went upstairs.

Ramadhin opened the door even before we knocked. We found Chintamoni sitting next to the open window. He said eagerly, 'Byomkesh babu, I saw you on the street and recognized you. Please come in.'

Chintamoni's appearance did not match his voice on the

telephone. He was a dark, plump man. Looking at him sitting upright on his chair, it was difficult even to think that he was paralysed. We noticed that on a small table next to him was an expensive pair of binoculars.

Chintamoni said, 'First, what will you take—tea, cocoa, Ovaltine?'

Byomkesh said, 'We don't want anything right now. Did the police question you today?'

'Of course! The OC is attacking me first and then Shanta in that house. What do they want? They have asked the same questions fifty times. I am paralysed, but can I climb down the stairs? Why do I have binoculars? Why did I rent out the house to Tapan? What answers can I give to these questions, tell me? I am tired of answering the same questions over and over again. Please, save me from them.'

Byomkesh said, 'Don't worry, everything will be fine. I have to meet the OC once. Will he...' Before Byomkesh could complete his sentence, the OC was at the door.

We had met Bijoy Bhaduri about ten years ago, when he was a junior police officer. He was shapeless and tall like a bamboo tree, but very active and had a very suspicious nature. I noticed that he had not changed a bit in all these years, although he had become an OC. That he was as suspicious as before was evident from the expression in his eyes.

He observed us sharply from the doorway and then entered the room. He said in a dry voice, 'Byomkesh babu!'

Byomkesh smiled and said, 'You have been able to recognize me. So, has your criminal Tapan Sen been arrested?'

Bijoy looked sharply at Chintamoni before saying, 'No, he has not been caught as yet, but where will he go? But what are you here for, Byomkesh babu?'

Byomkesh said, 'Chintamoni babu is my client. The murder

took place near his house, his tenant is the murderer, so the police are harassing him. He has employed me to rescue him from all this trouble.'

Bijoy looked at Byomkesh with sharp, questioning eyes, probably considering throwing him out of the house! But when he spoke again, his voice and attitude had completely changed. He bent towards Byomkesh and said in a low voice, 'Could you come outside? I wish to talk to you.'

'Okay.'

We went out and stood at one corner of the long verandah outside. Bijoy said with a forced smile, 'Look Byomkesh babu, you have great influence with the higher ranks; if you wish to interfere in this case, I cannot stop you. But I am requesting you, don't try to help Chintamoni Kundu. I firmly believe that he and his servant are involved in this case.'

Byomkesh listened to him attentively and then said, 'Do you know who committed the murder?'

Bijoy said, 'Definitely, Tapan Sen is the culprit, but that old fellow is also involved.'

'If the old fellow is involved, then would he have reported the murder to the police and accused Tapan Sen?'

'That is his cunning plot, he wants to get Tapan arrested and go scot-free himself.'

Byomkesh said in an irritated tone, 'Sorry, Bijoy babu, you have not understood a thing in this case.'

Frowning angrily, Bijoy said, 'What do you mean?'

Byomkesh said, 'I'll explain what I mean later. First, answer a few of my questions. Did you get the knife with which the crime was committed?'

'No, Tapan ran away with it.'

'Did you get anything after searching Tapan's house?'

'No, we did not get anything that would give us a clue as

to where he had fled. But we haven't opened the iron safe, the key is with Tapan.'

'Did you get any clue after questioning Shanta?'

'Nothing important. They were married about four months back. She does not seem to know anything about her husband's activities.'

'All right, but I know everything. I know who has committed the murder. I also know where the culprit is hiding.'

Bijoy jumped up, 'Why didn't you say so till now?'

Byomkesh smiled, 'I'll reveal everything in time. But before that, I want to see Tapan's house once. Also, I want to ask Shanta a few questions. You have interrogated her and must have gotten satisfactory answers. I'll ask her only a few questions.'

Bijoy said, 'All right, but the culprit?'

'You will get the culprit too.'

'Where? In that house? I can't understand what you are saying!'

'You will understand everything soon. Now let us go to that house. Be ready to catch the criminal.'

'What do you mean? Do you mean to say that Tapan will come back to his house? Or, is he hiding in that house?'

'Come, come,' Byomkesh began to lead the way down the stairs. Before that, he stood outside the doorway of Chintamoni's room and said, 'Don't be afraid, Chintamoni babu. We are going to that house and within an hour, we will crack the case.'

Then we went downstairs.

Tapan's house was surrounded by policemen. I have always noticed that the police become more vigilant after the thief escapes. What is the use of guarding the house when the culprit has escaped, I wondered! Byomkesh walked through the alley to the back door of the house.

Before reaching the back door, Byomkesh said, 'Is there no

way to escape, except through the front and back doors? What about scaling the wall?'

Bijoy said, 'No, no other way.'

There was a policeman guarding the back door; it was still locked. Bijoy asked the policeman to open the lock. We went inside.

A small compound inside led to two rooms—a kitchen on one side and the washroom. Byomkesh said, 'Bijoy babu, you and Ajit go in and sit with Shanta; I will have a look at the kitchen and the washroom.'

I entered the front room with Bijoy. It was a seating room with a cane furniture set. Shanta was sitting helplessly on a cane chair, looking desolate. Chintamoni's description of the young woman was very accurate. Now her hair was uncombed and her eyes were swollen, it looked as if she had been weeping.

She lifted her head when we entered and looked questioningly at Bijoy. The latter said nothing but sat on a chair, as did I.

The three of us sat silently. I felt that the girl was tired with the constant interrogation by the police. Even if she was innocent and had no connection with her husband's crime, she won't be spared by the guardians of law! But why did Tapan kill that man? Was it sexual jealousy? Did Shanta have some relationship with the victim?

Byomkesh was smiling to himself as he entered the room through the bedroom. He pulled up a chair in front of Shanta and kept looking at her with a smiling face.

Shanta, too, looked up at him with tired eyes, then, as she saw him smiling away, her expression suddenly changed to one of fear and alertness.

She sat up and asked hesitatingly, 'What... What?'

Byomkesh said in a pleasant voice, 'I saw a small iron safe in your bedroom. What is inside it?'

Shanta said, 'I told the OC I don't know what is inside it. My husband always keeps the keys with himself.'

Bijoy said, 'I have made arrangements to break the lock of the iron safe.'

'Good, good!' Byomkesh sounded unusually happy. 'You will get a lot of stuff there—the loot of all the daylight robberies—ornaments, cash, etc.' Then, turning to Shanta, he said, 'Just tell me one thing, didn't your husband shave? I could not find any shaving apparatus here.'

Shanta turned pale. She said in a low voice, 'He used to shave in the salon.'

Byomkesh said, 'I see. Your husband was an exceptional character. He used to shave in the salon; he never used sandals at home. Was there any reason for that?'

Shanta lowered her eyes and said, 'His sandals had torn, he hadn't bought a new pair as yet. He used to wear mine at home.'

Byomkesh said, 'Really? That means yours and his sizes were the same.'

Shanta said, 'Yes, nearly the same.'

Byomkesh said, 'Great! How convenient! You and your husband had a lot of similarities. Only the colour of your hair were different. Chintamoni babu told us that Tapan's hair was copper coloured, isn't it?'

Shanta swallowed hard and said, 'Yes.'

Bijoy was listening wide-eyed to the conversation. He suddenly stood up in great excitement and said, 'Byomkesh babu...!'

Byomkesh lifted his hand and said, 'Wait, be ready. This is my last question—Chintamoni babu had seen a red mole on your cheek. Where is it?'

Shanta quickly touched her left cheek, then composed herself and said, 'Mole? What mole? I don't have any mole on my cheek. Chintamoni babu must have been mistaken; maybe that day, I had a red ink mark there.'

Byomkesh gave a ferocious smile as he said, 'You seem to have an answer for every question. But what will you answer for this one?' He pulled at Shanta's hair in a quick movement, and at once, the wig she was wearing fell off, exposing her short, reddish hair!

Shanta, too, acted very fast. She bent down a little, lifted her saree from her left leg, revealing a sharp, thin knife attached to her leg with elastic bands. She pulled it out as quick as lightning and would have plunged it into Byomkesh's throat, if Bijoy had not been faster than her. He lunged at her like a tiger and held her hand in a tight grip. The knife fell on the floor. Paralysed with fear, I watched the whole episode, as if in a nightmare. A good-looking, soft-spoken woman changed, in no time, into a harsh, ugly killer—this was unimaginable. Now, rendered totally helpless, she was hissing away like a snake.

If Bijoy was not ready, then Byomkesh would surely have been killed by the woman. Byomkesh stood up smiling, 'This is your culprit, and that is the weapon with which the crime was committed!'

Bijoy, who was trying to recover from the suddenness of the whole incident, said hesitatingly, 'But Chintamoni was saying that Tapan Sen…'

Byomkesh said, 'There is no existence of Tapan Sen, Bijoy babu! There is only Shanta Sen; she is Tapan Sen at night and Shanta Sen by day. She is the one and only, a great lady, man and woman embodied in one; and don't think that her only crime was to kill Bidhubhushan Aich! About two months back, she had escaped from Burdwan Jail by killing a guard. I don't know her real name. You are in the police force, you may know the name of this escaped, fugitive criminal!'

Bijoy held Shanta's hand in a tight grip, glared at her angrily and said in a threatening voice, 'Promila Pal! Now I have understood everything. You were given life imprisonment for poisoning your husband. After two years of jail, you killed the guard and escaped. You came here incognito and acted as both husband and wife, very cleverly hoodwinking everyone. Then that fateful night, Bidhubhushan saw you and recognized you. He followed you to track you down and you killed him mercilessly near your house.' Bijoy looked at Byomkesh and said, 'This is the story, isn't it?'

Byomkesh said, 'Yes, more or less.'

Bijoy called the other policemen and asked them to handcuff Pramila Pal.

∽

Later, while sipping tea at Chintamoni babu's house, Byomkesh said, 'I had my doubts after reading your letter. You had never seen the two of them together, and even with your binoculars, you could not make out anything inside their house—why? The man was short and the woman was tall. They do not use the front door but the back door. The man talks in a hoarse voice—why? I felt that there was some hide and seek going on.

'There is no need to go into detail. The main fact is that after escaping from the jail, Promila Pal needed two things—a disguise and livelihood. She had reddish coloured hair—which attracted attention—so she cut it short, like a man's. But to rob the poor housewives during the day, she had to be a woman. So, she procured a beautiful wig. Thus began her dual life. It is winter now, so it is easy for a female to dress as a male. She wore a butterfly moustache, wore an overcoat on top of shirt and trousers, and then came to you to ask for the house. In case her voice sounded feminine, she spoke in a hoarse voice. It is easy to move around in a disguise in Calcutta, as everyone is so busy here that they are not bothered about their neighbours' affairs. But she noticed that you had a pair of binoculars, and also that you noticed everything while sitting beside your window. So she had to be extra careful.

'That night, she occupied the house after you had gone to bed. No one knew how many people had taken the house or occupied it—one or two? She had an iron safe with her, which she kept in her bedroom.

'Then she started her daily life. She went out in the morning, saying that she taught in a school. At noon, she planned and robbed poor, unsuspecting housewives by entering the houses in the guise of a saleswoman. She then returned in the afternoon, dressed up like a man and went out in the evening to dupe you. She switched off the electric light and lighted a lamp, which went off after sometime when the oil was finished. You thought that Shanta had put out the light and gone off to sleep. You made one mistake—you did not realize that the electric lights went off before Tapan, not Shanta, went out in the evening. You were not suspicious, so you had no doubt in your mind. After you went off to sleep, she would come back quietly, enter through the back door and sleep. For safety's sake, she carried a shawl to cover herself. So on the first night when you saw her returning, covered in a shawl, you thought that it was Shanta's lover with whom she was having a secret affair.

'Things were going along in this manner. But suddenly, Promila was in great danger. Bidhubhushan Aich was a police officer from Burdwan, the place from where Promila had escaped. He had come to Calcutta on leave. He saw and recognized Promila in spite of her disguise. He followed her...and the rest is history.'

Byomkesh lighted a cigarette. I said, 'Why didn't she escape after murdering Bidhubhushan?'

Byomkesh said, 'Where did she get the time? Chintamoni babu had seen the entire episode of her murdering him and had immediately called the police. She had not bargained for that. She had planned to escape with all her loot, but the police came and surrounded the house. There was no way to escape, so she put on her wig and pretended to be Tapan's wife. But in her haste, she forgot to put on the reddish mole on her left cheek! She used the mole to make a difference between Tapan and Shanta.'

Getting up, he said, 'All right, Chintamoni babu, we will take your leave now.'

Chintamoni was very grateful—he thanked us and rewarded Byomkesh with a fat cheque. We started on our way back home.

It was nearly two o'clock. The police had left with the culprit. Bijoy would surely take all the credit from his seniors for capturing the criminal.

When we reached home, we found Satyabati waiting anxiously for us. She lifted her eyebrows, 'Why so late?'

Byomkesh suddenly started laughing heartily, then touched her chin affectionately and said, 'Kudos to you, ladies!'

Acknowledgements

I would like to convey my heartfelt gratitude to my husband, Prof. P.P. Dhar, for his support and hard work in typing out the stories, correcting errors in the manuscript and his constructive criticism; and to Rupa Publications for making it possible to publish the stories.